D1298305

Women of the Passion

a novel   Joan D. Lynch

MSJ PRESS

Women of the Passion

a novel
Joan D. Lynch

Publishing Manager: Andrew Yankech
Cover Design, Book Design, and Typesetting: Michael Babin
Cover Artwork: Mary Southard, CSJ

Copyright © 2010 by Joan D. Lynch. All rights reserved.

Published by MSJ Press, Naples, Florida
www.WomenOfThePassionANovel.com

WOMEN OF THE PASSION is distributed by:
ACTA Publications, 4848 N. Clark Street, Chicago, IL 60640
(800) 397-2282, www.actapublications.com

WOMEN OF THE PASSION is a work of fiction. Names, characters, places, and incidents are the products of the author's imagination or are used fictitiously.

All rights reserved. No part of this publication may be reproduced or transmitted in any form or by any means, electronic or mechanical, including photocopying or recording, or by any information storage and retrieval system, including the Internet, without permission from the publisher, except in the case of brief quotations with proper citation in critical analysis or reviews.

Library of Congress Number: 2010940129
ISBN: 978-0-9829640-0-2
Printed in the United States of America on recycled paper
Year: 15 14 13 12 11 10
Printing: 05 04 03 02 First Edition

To my husband Tom for his unflagging support, my daughter Julie for her special insights, and my family and friends for their encouragement and help at every stage of the process.

*T*HEY HAD TRAVELED *with him, witnessed his miracles, and listened to his teachings. Now, on a hill called Golgotha, they stand at the foot of the cross on which he hangs. This is the story of the women of the Passion and the men who take that journey with them.*

Chapter One

ARY MAGDALENE'S ARM is growing numb from the weight of the mother. She adjusts it, careful not to jar the dazed woman, who now looks much older than her forty-seven years. She notices that the lines on Mary's face have deepened, and her eyes are rimmed by deep circles. She feels John, who is on Mary's other side, also adjust his arm. *What a blessing these distractions are,* she thinks. But she knows she can't keep her eyes on the ruddy soil, bloodied from so many daily crucifixions. She has to look into his eyes once more, see his pain, and feel his love—perhaps for the last time.

She raises her head and looks at the handsome, still muscular man who hangs before her. As their eyes meet he says pleadingly, "I thirst." She looks over at the centurion and wordlessly begs for his help. The soldiers around him sneer, but the centurion mercifully responds, jabbing a sponge with his javelin, soaking it in wine, and raising it up to Jesus' mouth. It grazes his cracked lips; his tongue reaches out for the liquid, and once again their eyes lock. She sees he wants something from her. *What? I have given him my utmost devotion these last three years. I have followed him everywhere, provided for him and his followers out of my own pocket, and watched him heal and even bring people back from death. He can do anything—even go willingly to this ignominious crucifixion. But why?* She still can't understand.

The sky darkens. Now the three crosses, his and those of the two thieves flanking him, are silhouetted against the sky. She feels a surge of anger break through her sorrow. The Romans chose to hang him between two common criminals. *And why did they label him the "King of the Jews"? He was the king of the whole world. Were they being sarcastic or was it a way to get back at the chief priests, who had insisted on his execution?*

*O*N THE OTHER side of Golgotha, a man makes his way up the hill. He moves stealthily, hoping to be forgotten by everyone—including his own conscience. Peter is a stocky, simple fisherman from Galilee who has never truly felt at ease among the sophisticated Jerusalem crowd. His slight speech impediment makes him even shier.

Yet Jesus saw something in me. No one ever believed in me like that, Peter recalls. Around Jesus, Peter had felt taller, freer, and more articulate. He had been immensely proud that Jesus had groomed him to be a leader. Empowered by Jesus, he had felt strong enough to face anything.

And yet when the Romans had come, he had turned his back on his Master. He had run away, driven by a deep-seated, unfathomable terror. But shame eventually had caught up with him and made him head to Golgotha.

It is too late, of course, he thinks, *but still here I am.*

Haggard, disheveled and tormented, Peter walks against the flow of onlookers who have had enough of the grim spectacle. He averts his face as they pass. *Strong, me? What a joke!* he thinks. *I have all the heart of a timid desert rat.*

Peter notices that most of the people are quiet and sad as they head back to town, but one small group had come to jeer and mock.

One of them laughs saying, "He saved others, but he can't save himself."

"Some King of the Jews!" a second man jeers.

Peter winces as they mock, clenching his fists tightly and thinking how much he would love to give them the thrashing they deserve.

Close enough now, he sees the three crosses uphill, and in the middle—Jesus is hanging. He stops behind a large rock and stares, horrified.

*M*ARY MAGDALENE WATCHES as the soldiers cast lots for his bloodied, dirty garments.

"See how it's done, boys," one of the soldiers calls out. He then casts his lot. "There! Hand over the robe."

A second soldier laughs contemptuously, "That rag? It'll look good on you." They all laugh. The winner jauntily throws the robe over his shoulders.

Mary, Jesus' mother, strangles a sob. "I made him that robe," she whispers to Mary Magdalene who gazes at her compassionately.

The soldiers cheer the winner. Mary Magdalene looks at them with disgust and then gasps as she watches a pregnant young girl, Miriam, break away from two expensively dressed older women—the short, portly Susanna and the tall, stately Joanna. She sees Susanna grab Miriam's arm and hears her say, "Let it be, Miriam."

Miriam shakes Susanna off and heads toward the winner. Mary Magdalene notices the alarmed look on the older women's faces and feels her own anxiety mount as she sees Miriam run toward the soldiers who roar in delight.

"How much for the robe?" Miriam says, proffering some coins to the winning soldier.

Making the most of this break in the monotony of the death watch, the soldier says expansively, "See, boys? The lady knows quality!"

Mary Magdalene watches the other soldiers laugh and crowd around the couple.

The soldier slowly in a voice filled with innuendo says, "What's it to you?"

Miriam pulls her cloak tightly around her and lowers her head. "Just sentimental," she replies.

"Sentimental, eh?" The soldier leers. "Did he leave you a souvenir?"

With that Mary Magdalene gasps as the soldier reaches to grope Miriam's pregnant belly. Miriam intercepts his hand, slaps the coins in it, and grabs the robe. The soldiers laugh.

"Only a fifteen-year-old would risk her life by doing what Miriam did," Mary Magdalene observes, "but then, she isn't an ordinary fifteen-year-old."

Mary Magdalene watches Miriam fold the garment hurriedly, hide it under her cloak, and rejoin the others. Joanna and Susanna look at her disapprovingly and throw their arms around her protectively.

*I*N THE FADING light, Peter can't see the commotion at Jesus' feet. All he hears is the Roman soldiers' braying laughter. The thought of it makes his blood boil. *What am I doing here, paralyzed, while these animals insult him?* Peter thinks. *Enough is enough.* He has to see for himself. He has to confront his cowardice.

Peter starts out from the shadows but beats a quick retreat when he sees a familiar figure approaching from the other side. He thinks, *What's Joseph doing here?*

He watches Joseph of Arimathea, an older, bearded, richly dressed man, hurry toward the place of execution. Peter knows that even though Joseph was a member of the Sanhedrin, he became a disciple of Jesus after listening to his preaching in Judea. Joseph was a secret disciple because he knew too well what the Sanhedrin thought about Jesus. Peter is shocked as he watches Joseph shed his self-protective nature. Joseph seems absolutely compelled and emboldened to move forward.

SEEING JOSEPH GO directly to the centurion in charge and take him aside, Mary Magdalene is surprised. *This is so unlike him,* she thinks. *When he heard Jesus was coming to Jerusalem, he went discreetly back to Arimathea. He didn't want to get involved with the high priests' vendetta against Jesus. So why is he here now?*

She watches him show a papyrus scroll to the centurion who reads it and frowns. He speaks animatedly to Joseph but finally nods his assent. *Whatever it is, this can't be easy for Joseph, a man who much prefers to melt into a crowd,* Mary realizes, incredibly moved by his efforts. Joseph comes toward them after he finishes with the Roman. As he gets closer, Mary can see the grief etched in his features.

He kisses Jesus' mother, who is grateful that he is here, and then stands beside Mary Magdalene.

Just then Jesus cries out in a loud voice, "My God, my God, why have you forsaken me?"

Mary Magdalene feels the older woman stiffen as she watches her son in agony and cries out piercingly, "Oh God, my God!"

Through her tears, Mary Magdalene sees the sky darken further. Although there is loud thunder and lightning that speeds across the sky in huge bolts, there's no rain. She wonders if this is a sign from God.

She notices the Romans have seen it, too, and they're clearly unnerved. They look up fearfully as the lightning crashes toward the crowd, and they cover their heads in terror. Mary Magdalene hears some of the women wail and sees them cover their eyes with their shawls. But her eyes remain riveted on Jesus.

"It is finished," she hears him say.

She wonders if this means that his work here on earth has been accomplished or that his death is its completion. Then a terrible sorrow erupts in her chest, which drives all thought from her mind. She sees Jesus look up to heaven, and she hears him say in a loud voice, "Father, into your hands I commit my spirit." As she begins to sob uncontrollably, she feels the earth shake. She struggles not to lose her footing and to continue holding up Mary, who has collapsed between John and her. All around her people are falling. She watches the centurion turn to his soldiers who are cowering in fear.

"This man was innocent," she hears him tell them.

Mary Magdalene sees the soldiers, who are trying to maintain their footing, come forward and break the legs of the two criminals. Alarmed, she thinks, *They're trying to hasten their deaths.*

As they walk toward Jesus, she screams loudly, "Don't!"

She waits to see what they will do as they look at Jesus. They see that he is already dead so, to Mary Magdalene's relief, they don't bother to break his legs. She watches as one soldier turns back and maliciously thrusts his lance into Jesus' side. Blood and water flow out. She starts to rush toward Jesus but she feels a calming hand on her shoulder. She turns to see Joseph.

"Let me," he says.

Wiping her tears, she watches as Joseph of Arimathea silently approaches the centurion with the burial cloths in hand. The centurion motions to the soldiers who lift the cross out and lay it on the ground. The other women move closer as the soldiers roughly pull the nails out. She covers Mary's eyes so that Jesus' mother won't see the gaping holes on her beloved son's wrists and ankles.

Mary Magdalene sees Joseph offer Mary the winding cloths and move forward with John. They lift Jesus' now limp body and bring it to his mother who sits on the ground to receive it. Mary Magdalene sobs as she realizes that this is the last time Mary will hold her son. She watches as tears stream down the mother's face as she kisses her son tenderly.

Tearfully, Mary motions to Mary Magdalene, who kisses his lips and blows warm air into his cold flesh as though she is trying to breathe life in him. She turns and helps Mary gently wrap him as they would a baby.

"His sufferings are over," Mary Magdalene tells his mother.

"I wish I were going to the Father with him," Mary answers, numbly.

Leading the group, Mary Magdalene with five of the women help John and Joseph carry the body by lending their shoulders on either side. The other women follow them in solemn procession. As she feels the weight, Mary Magdalene loses herself in thought. *I wonder if this is what his cross felt like as he made his way to Calvary.*

Wrapping and carrying him, these practical tasks ease the terrible sorrow. The group moves on to what has been an unseen part of the hill. It is a graveyard with many tombs cut into the rocks and sealed by large stone wheels.

As Mary Magdalene moves past these graves, her grief intensifies as she remembers her parents laid to rest in a similar grave in Magdala. As if to offer her some hope, she notices the vegetation change from tall grasses to a carpet of flowers; her favorites, red and white anemones; alternating with sky blue sword lilies, purple crowfoot, lilac, and white asphodel.

Led by Joseph, they enter into the darkness of an open tomb and lay the body on the stone slab. Mary Magdalene feels the sudden cold and shivers.

"We'll come after the Sabbath to wash the body and anoint it," she says to Joseph in a low voice.

Joseph nods. She then encourages Mary to kiss her son one last time. Mary Magdalene watches as Jesus' mother sits on the slab beside him and lays her head on his chest. She and the others avert their eyes to give the mother this last moment of privacy.

As the mourners honor their dead leader, Mary Magdalene helps Mary out of the dark space. She notices that the light is fading and thinks, *It will only be minutes before the start of Sabbath. I always look forward to Sabbath, but this one will be long and impossibly empty without Jesus.* She looks around at her fellow disciples; they seem equally lost without their Master.

The sun rims the horizon as the men wheel the stone in place to seal the tomb. Mary grasps Joseph's arm and thanks him for all he has done.

"You are a good and kind man."

Joseph bows his head and says softly, "I loved Jesus also."

"You are a very brave man," Mary Magdalene tells Joseph. "How will we ever repay you?"

"Being here is payment enough, but now I must go back to Arimathea."

Mary nods. "I understand." She realizes that they won't see Joseph again.

Mary Magdalene watches the other women all murmur their thanks as well. She sees John kiss Mary goodbye, embrace Joseph, and then lope back up the hill toward Golgotha.

Mary Magdalene feels someone lean over toward her. She turns to see Joanna who asks, "Do you think Peter might be up there?"

"John would know that," Mary Magdalene replies. "The two of them are so close."

Suddenly, Mary hears Salome—wrinkled, gap-toothed, and bent—call out, "John, my son!" All eyes turn to the old woman.

Mary Magdalene sees John freeze and start back. She can tell from the look on his face his stomach is churning with resentment.

"Yes, Mother," he says, blushing. Mary Magdalene sees that he is embarrassed when his mother exerts her claim on him. She know that Salome is proud of John's place so close to Jesus and wonders if Salome is ashamed that her other son, James, was not with them as well.

Mary watches Salome gaze up at John adoringly, "Take care of yourself. There may still be Romans up there."

"I will, Mother."

*J*OHN TURNS AND retraces his steps, climbing up to Golgotha. His mother's interruption reminds him powerfully of her asking Jesus for her two sons to sit at his right and left when he came into his kingdom. Today Jesus had come into his kingdom, not in the blaze of glory that they had anticipated but in an ignominious crucifixion. He remembers Jesus' words about how among the pagans, great men make their authority felt, but in Jesus' world, the great must be the servants of many. A person who wishes to be the first must be the slave of all. Jesus' words from that night echo in his head, "The Son of Man came not to be served but to serve and to give his life for the ransom of many." *Jesus had known he would suffer,* John thinks, *but* *we only now realize the extent of what he would have to endure.*

When John reaches the top of the hill, he sees that the soldiers are gone and Jesus' empty cross lies on the ground. The other two crosses are tossed one on top of the other. Then he sees a lone figure, staring down the side of the hill. He calls out for Peter in a low voice. John watches Peter turn and motion for him to come over. He sees Peter's bleary eyes and then stares into the pit on the side of Golgotha at a pile of bleached white bones and skulls. The bodies of the two criminals had been thrown on top by the soldiers and are now being torn apart by jackals.

"This would have been Jesus' fate, if Joseph of Arimathea hadn't intervened," he hears Peter mumble.

John's stomach lurches and, eyes closed, he dry heaves, imagining the horror. John notices that Peter can't take his eyes off the pit.

He speaks haltingly—as he always does when nervous. "I was a coward. I don't have the courage of a woman."

John touches Peter. "Jesus named you 'The Rock' and appointed you the leader of his followers."

Peter shakes his hand off and turns to him. "I am Simon, the Sponge! Anyone can wring me out—even a maidservant."

A loud rumble of thunder and then a crash of lightning frighten the men.

"What's to stop the Romans from killing us, too?" Peter asks.

John shakes his head and says softly, "Jesus can. He said he'd rise in three days."

"Then he will lead the disciples!" John watches Peter drop his head into his hands and then suddenly look up. "We are wanted men. If we surface, we'll be killed as revolutionaries. It's best if we go back to Galilee." John looks at him sadly as he continues to spew out his fear, "I'm the wrong person to lead. Putting my nets down and hauling in the fish—that's what I can do."

"Jesus believes in you."

"He's through with me. I'm nothing, a nobody. Don't you see?"

PETER COVERS HIS ears as he remembers the loud crow of a cock in the yard of the high priest. Accosted by a maid and accused of being a follower of Jesus, he had denied him not once but three times. Shame fills him as he remembers the details of this betrayal and his vehement denial to her. *Jesus wouldn't want anything more to do with me if he knew.*

"I betrayed him just as surely as Judas did." Peter looked up to heaven with tears coursing down his cheeks. "So you believe he will rise from the dead? How will I face him then?"

"He will forgive you as he always has."

"Why did he choose me?"

The squawk of the buzzards that are now circling the pit interrupts them.

"It'll be dark soon," John urges. "Let's join the others. Are they still at Susanna's?"

Peter mutters, "Maybe."

Another flash of lightning is followed by hard rain. They look up fearfully.

John says, "I hope the women don't get caught in this."

$\mathcal{M}$ARY MAGDALENE FEELS the cold sting of the rain as it soaks her cloak. She draws Mary closer to her when she feels the older woman shiver. The street is becoming increasingly more muddy and slippery. She watches Joanna, who is in front of her, hold up Salome after she stumbles and then falls in the mud. Mary Magdalene observes Joanna examine Salome's hand, which is bleeding. *How strong and dependable Joanna is*, Mary Magdalene thinks, *What a support she's been to us.* Mary Magdalene remembers how Joanna had walked with them the last three years when her duties at court had permitted. *Her husband, Chuza, Herod's steward, has always been grateful that Jesus had healed his beloved. I am so thankful for her generous heart and how she has used her ample funds to take care of us, and even now, in her lowest hour and as bereft as she is, she still gives of herself.*

As they reach the outskirts of the city, Mary Magdalene looks longingly at the comfortable, well-appointed house she sees in the distance. Joanna and Chuza had inherited it from his mother, and Joanna had always sheltered the single women there when they had needed a place to stay in Jerusalem. The stone dwelling was more prosperous looking than those around it. Mary Magdalene smiles as she remembers the joyous times they had known there when it had been a stop on their journey.

The women struggle up the steps. Mary Magdalene watches Joanna open the door, and the warmth of the room envelops them. Her eyes drift to the high wood-framed windows cut in the stone walls, and then to the main room, dimly lit, furnished simply with a table, some chairs, trunks, and a pile of pillows in an attractive fabric in one corner.

Mary Magdalene sees Joanna help Salome, the oldest of the women, off with her wet cloak. Mary Magdalene takes a pale and feverish Mary to the back of the room; unrolls her bedroll; and, gently after removing her cloak, lays her down. She notices that Mary's cloak, which usually serves as a blanket, is soaked. She turns to see that Joanna has anticipated this and hands her a blanket. Mary Magdalene thanks Joanna who moves back to Salome with another blanket in hand.

Kneeling, Mary Magdalene kisses Mary's sorrowful face and asks the question which had haunted her throughout this long painful day, "Why, Mother?"

"He said yes to God."

"As you did."

Mary Magdalene looks lovingly at Jesus' mother, and she nods. The two women hold each other and sob.

$\mathcal{T}$WO OTHER WOMEN haven't reached home yet. They are still struggling through the shadowy late afternoon, dense with soaking rain. Miriam looks up at the portly Susanna. She feels Susanna holding her up with her powerful arms. They both worry that she will slip and injure herself and the baby. Miriam groans. The distance to Susanna's home, in which she houses the men, has never seemed this long. She knows they are both tired, and that Susanna's legs, which never rest from dawn to dusk in the service of others, must feel wooden now. Miriam can tell that Susanna is forcing herself to push on.

Miriam, hugging Jesus' robe close to her swollen belly, thinks, *If only I had had this when my father lay dying, I would have placed it on him and surely he would have been healed.* Fresh tears spring into her eyes as one death merges with the other. The pain engulfs her, making her fear for the life of her baby. *Surely he must feel this, too,* she thinks. Suddenly the rain stops, she looks up. *Perhaps that is a good omen, and my baby is still safe.*

$\mathcal{M}$ARY MAGDALENE CLOSES the door to Joanna's house softly behind her so as not to awaken the sleeping women inside. Across the narrow street, she sees a large, bountiful meadow filled with fruit trees.

The heavy rains have cleansed the close Jerusalem air, and the fragrant scent of ripe fruit from the orchard assaults her. She remembers the dusty air of Golgotha that had carried with it the smell of blood and sweat. This fragrance seems a rebuke to Jesus' suffering. *Couldn't the earth remain in mourning just a little while longer? Why must it recover so quickly?* She feels the mud ooze between her bare toes as she crosses to the meadow crowded with fig and olive trees. The fallen figs cut into her bare feet. The pain is welcome, diverting her from the internal all-consuming pain. Exhausted, she sits at the foot of a tree, absentmindedly brushing her hand over some of the fallen fruits. She picks up one of them—its skin torn open and flesh spilling out as though it too had been disemboweled by a Roman lance. The moment her fingers touch the wounded flesh, she breaks down into deep sobs and cries out, "I wish I'd died with him." Her face wet with tears, she slides to the ground under the tree, unmindful of the soaked earth beneath her.

*I*NSIDE THE UPSTAIRS room of Susanna's large, imposing stone house, the men are tense. Nine of the apostles have gathered here, including Peter's brother Andrew, Matthew, Thomas, James the Elder, Philip, and James the Younger. Four disciples are with them. One of them, Cleopas, the husband of Miriam, paces in great agitation. On a normal day, Cleopas would have marveled at the size of this rooftop room with its magnificent semicircular windows and heavy architectural detail. But today wasn't a normal day, and his focus was listening for the women's footsteps on one of the two staircases leading up to the room.

A knock on the outside door startles the men.

"Who's there?" Matthew standing by the door, whispers.

"Susanna and Miriam," Cleopas hears the faint, seemingly exhausted reply.

He looks frantically at Matthew, who glances back at the other men and nods affirmatively. Cleopas rushes to the door, pulls back the heavy bar, opens it, and clutches the bedraggled Miriam in his arms. They both begin to cry.

"I've been so worried about you," Cleopas says. "Have you had anything to eat or drink?"

Miriam shakes her head.

"What about our baby? Didn't you think about our baby?"

Miriam whispers, "I only thought about Jesus."

Cleopas helps her lie on his mat. Reaching for a pitcher of water and a towel, he tenderly washes his wife's face. He watches as his kind touch causes her face to crumble, and his heart breaks as she pours out her grief and fears in great wracking sobs. Cleopas looks to the men in the room, who are still and silent as they watch him take care of his wife.

"We'll stay here another day, so you can regain your strength," Cleopas says anxiously, "but then I'm taking you home."

"Please, Cleopas, no! I'll be fine."

"Jerusalem is a tinder box, Miriam. It could erupt at any time."

"But I'd like Jesus' mother to deliver our baby. She's the best midwife in the whole area."

"I can't risk losing you just as you're about to give birth to our child."

As he tries to wash her hands, he sees Miriam is breaking down again.

Cleopas says tenderly, "What? What's wrong?"

"They pounded the nails into his wrists and feet."

Cleopas winces. The pain around the room is palpable.

LED BY ANDREW, the men who had been listening move to the other end of the long room. Susanna follows them and sits on a cushion at the far end. She takes off her soaking cloak and towels her wet hair. The rosiness that normally suffuses her cheeks begins to seep back. The men watch her, knowing it will be some time before the short, portly woman will regain her usual broad smile. They look at her expectantly. When she doesn't speak, Andrew breaks the silence.

"Who else was there?"

Susanna answers in a dull voice, "Mary Magdalene, Jesus' mother, Salome, Joanna..." Her voice trails off.

Shocked, Andrew asks, "Joanna, the wife of Herod's steward?"

Susanna nods. Andrew looks around at the others. Matthew speaks for the group. "What a brave woman."

James the Younger exclaims, "She'll be very lucky if they don't crucify her." The men nod in agreement.

James the Elder asks tentatively, "And my mother, Salome, was there?"

Susanna nods. James the Elder moves away from the group and sits dejectedly.

James the Younger asks, "Peter and John?"

"John was. I didn't see Peter."

The men look at one another in consternation.

"Perhaps he has been arrested," Matthew says. The others nod, indicating that they had been thinking the same thought.

Thomas breaks in urgently, "We should leave for Galilee as soon as John returns."

Philip agrees. "It's not safe here."

Thomas cries out vehemently, "They'll crucify us all."

"Thomas is right," Philip retorts. "Pilate's probably planning it already."

Many of the others murmur in agreement.

Pontius Pilate—the very name struck fear in the hearts of Jesus' disciples because as Rome's representative in Judea, he had the power to crucify. He had crucified their Lord, but he had been merely the apex of the power chain. The men knew beneath Pilate was Herod Antipas, the tetrarch of Galilee. He was one of three successors to his father, Herod the Great, who had divided his conquered realm into three parts, giving one to each of three sons. Further down the chain were those who were the real power to whom the people bowed: the high priests headed by a chief and the

Sanhedrin, seventy men who served as an advisory court. The high priests feared Jesus, and now they had sent him to his death.

LATE ON THIS fateful day, Pilate sits on a throne-like chair in the sumptuous palace that had been built by Herod the Great for his stays in Jerusalem. Pilate reflects, *How fitting it is that the finest of the palaces have been given to me, the conqueror. The throne room's marble walls and the floor's complex mosaic are elegant. The fountains and gardens both surrounding the palace and inside the inner courtyard are so extravagant; the rhythmic spray of the water calms my spirit.*

Today Pilate knows he needs calming because he has visitors— unwelcome visitors. *They have the power to notify Rome of slights, real or imagined, that could get me summoned to Rome,* he thinks indignantly. *What a terror-filled experience that would be, especially when the man I report to is Caligula! I don't want much. I just want to hold on to my position until my wife, Claudia, and I can go back to Rome and retire—in splendor, perhaps in a villa outside the city.*

For this audience, Pilate, a tall man with an aquiline nose, is dressed in his most expensive toga, trimmed with gold leaf. He watches as his soldiers open the massive doors. The chief priest, Caiaphas, and his father-in-law; Annas, a former chief priest; enter the room followed by ten other priests, members of the Sanhedrin. *Today,* Pilate notes, *they have chosen to come in their priestly*

*robes—always a bad sign—because what they want, I may not want
to give.* As they proceed down the long aisle to his throne, he feels
the familiar mixture of fear and dislike for these power-mongering
sycophants. *Yes, they will bow and scrape,* Pilate remembers, *but
there is always a veiled threat that if they don't get what they want,
they will make me wish I had given it gladly.*

Both men before him are heavily bearded. Caiaphas, dark
haired, is powerfully built; Annas, white haired, is thin and crafty
looking. *They are a pair of rats,* Pilate thinks, *come out of their
holes to dine. Well not on me. Sorry but today you won't dine on
me. I've done enough dirty work for you.*

"What can I do for you today?" he asks them. "It must be very urgent
for you to come so close to the start of your *precious* Sabbath."

Annas opens, exclaiming in a strident voice, "Your Excellency,
you allowed that impostor to be buried."

Pilate bristles at the suggestion that he did something wrong.
Keeping his voice tightly under control, he asks, "What about it?"

Annas replies hotly, "He said that after three days he would rise."

Smiling, Pilate says sarcastically, "Come now, Annas, even you
can't believe that!"

"Of course I don't!"

"Then why are you so afraid of this man? He's been crucified!"

Caiaphas answers craftily, "His followers might take the body."

Annas chimes in again, "Then they could say he had risen as he
had prophesied."

"The situation would be worse than before," Caiaphas says in a measured tone.

Standing, Pilate speaks to them mockingly, "So you see a bunch of illiterate Galileans banding together to keep his name alive?"

Annas and Caiaphas nod. The men behind them murmur in agreement. Pilate shakes his head in disgust.

"Very well, I'll post guards—this time. But I'm through with this Jesus business, understand?" They nod. "I appointed you to keep *your* people in line."

The priests behind them look at each other in reaction to this new knowledge. Annas looks back at them and then at Caiaphas. Pilate notices their discomfort. He smiles.

"Don't make me do it for you again," Pilate growls.

Caiaphas, visibly trying to keep his fear in check, says, "We'd like to completely seal the tomb as well."

Pilate's voice now drips with sarcasm. "You do that. You're good at keeping things under wraps."

Chapter Two

*T*HE SABBATH HAS been an interminable, painful day for the women waiting in Joanna's house. The dark night has not been lightened by dawn yet, but a full moon shines enough light for the women to set out on their sacred task. The table is set like an altar with washcloths, a jar of water, a bowl of scented oil, and small blocks of myrrh and aloe. They move quietly as they put on their cloaks, fearful of waking Mary, who is lying asleep on a mat covered by a blanket and her dry cloak. She has slept fitfully throughout the long Sabbath. Mary Magdalene kneels and feels Mary's forehead.

"She's still feverish," she says to Joanna and Salome.

Moving quietly, the women each take an object from the table, light their torches, and exit into the faint light of the street. Mary Magdalene's heart beats fast as she anticipates seeing him again. Dead and lifeless, he is no less precious to her. It will ease her grief to wash his body and spread the fragrant oil, which she carries, on him. This is her last gift to him.

Carrying a lit torch and their burial objects, they walk silently, seemingly gliding through the deserted streets. Mary Magdalene knows each of them fears the encounter with the Roman soldiers at the Gate of the Gardens, but they are trying to keep their fears to themselves. She fortifies herself by thinking men would never hurt women on such a mission, but she knows the character of the Roman soldier, and so she begins to pray silently, *Dear God, let them allow us to pass unharmed. Whatever happens, Joanna and I are strong enough to handle it, but Salome is old and frightens easily.* The first glimmerings of the sun appear as Mary Magdalene spots the arch of the gate. *Dear Lord, please let these men be kind.* Armed with the prayer, she moves forward confidently and sees two soldiers at the gate.

The two Roman soldiers see the women approach. Mary Magdalene watches the taller, heavier one turn to the other.

"Marcus, look who's coming!"

"Doesn't look as if there's a man with them," the younger, fresh-faced one replies. "Leave them alone."

The first one smiles at him cockily. Overhearing the interaction, Mary Magdalene anxiously motions to the women to walk closer together and lower their heads as they reach the gate. The larger one moves to block the way.

"Where are you going?" he asks.

Without looking up, Mary Magdalene replies in a monotone, "To anoint a body for burial."

When there is no reply, Mary Magdalene looks up to see—the leering face of the older soldier. She closes her eyes against the searing image in her mind: the same soldier stretching Jesus' arm on the crossbeam and then hammering a nail into his wrist. With the sound of the hammered nail reverberating in her head, Mary Magdalene's face visibly whitens. Distracted, Mary Magdalene doesn't notice the soldier rudely grasp at the bowl in her hand.

"Let's see what you have," he exclaims as he wrests the bowl from her.

Mary Magdalene watches numbly as he puts his finger into the bowl, rubs the oil all over her face, and laughs at her consternation. Out of the corner of her eye, she sees the other women cower, but Mary Magdalene silently defies him. The precious oil runs down her face like tears. She notices the second solider walk up.

"Titus, I told you to leave them alone," the young soldier says boldly. He turns to her, "Pass."

"Marcus, you're ruining my game."

Mary Magdalene looks up at Marcus gratefully as she motions for the women to move cautiously around them. Mary Magdalene is so focused on the women that she doesn't see the first soldier lunge at her. Suddenly she feels him grab her hair and force her head back.

"You didn't like that? Then how about this?" he cackles as he pours oil over her head and then carelessly tosses the empty bowl away. "I anoint you first harlot. You have the right to do everything I tell you."

"You've had your fun," Marcus barks as he pushes his laughing compatriot away. "Let them go." The women move past as Titus calls out, "Maybe there'll be a crucifixion tomorrow."

Mary Magdalene trembles in rage as they walk away. She feels someone put an arm around her. She turns and sees Joanna's concerned face.

"Did he hurt you?"

"Not like he hurt my Lord."

The women enter the rocky area where the tombs are located. Mary Magdalene remembers the feel of his body on her shoulders and looks down at her empty hands. Now she doesn't even have the consolation of rubbing the oil into his cold skin. The myrrh and aloe that Joanna carries will have to suffice.

She hears someone quicken her step to catch up with her. There is a tug on her sleeve.

"What if there are soldiers at the tomb as well?" Salome asks. "They'll want to hurt us too. I don't want to go any farther."

Mary Magdalene answers soothingly, "They know our customs. They'll expect us to anoint him."

Joanna answers sarcastically, "Will they also roll back the stone for us?" Mary smiles at her friend's words.

Suddenly the earth shakes as it had at the crucifixion. Mary

Magdalene falls, clutching herself in fear, and watches Joanna do the same. She looks at the women's faces and sees that everyone is terrified. The women look at each other in bewilderment as a bright light emanates from the area of the tomb. Suddenly, Mary hears panicked shouts.

"I can't see! I can't see!" The women turn looking for the source of the cries. Two young Roman soldiers run away, with one leading the other, who is covering his eyes.

"I'm blind!" he cries.

Mary Magdalene sees something dart away behind her. She turns and watches Salome run in the other direction. Mary Magdalene runs after her, gently takes her arm, and leads her back to the group.

"Have courage," she says soothingly. "Let's see what has happened."

As they reach the tomb, they discover the stone rolled back and a blinding radiance emanating from within. Mary Magdalene takes it all in and is filled with wonder. *Can it be he?* she thinks as she looks around for a sign. *Who else then?* Mary Magdalene feels Salome pull her hand.

"I want to leave," Salome whispers fearfully.

Brushing her own fear aside, Mary Magdalene pushes them on. She encourages the women to enter the tomb. The first thing Mary sees is a beautiful, androgynous angel seated on the stone bench where Jesus had been and bathed in radiant light. Beside him are the wrappings that had been on Jesus, including the cloth still in the shape of his head. Mary Magdalene gazes at them, thinking, *Where is he? Where has he gone?* She falls to her knees and bows her head to the floor. She hears the rustle of clothing as the other women do the same.

"Why are you looking for the living among the dead?" the angel asks. The women look up in astonishment, covering their eyes from the angel's blinding light. "He's walking among you."

Suddenly, the angel disappears, but his radiance fills the tomb. Stunned, Mary Magdalene repeats the words in her head, *"He's walking among you. He's walking among you. He's walking among you." Where? Dear God, let me see him.*

$\mathcal{T}$HE WARM GLOW of the sunrise washes over the women as they exit the tomb. Mary Magdalene looks at each woman's face and sees that they are reeling in amazement. Joanna walks up to her and whispers, "My God!"

In awe, Mary Magdalene replies, "We've been blessed!"

"Mary," Salome rushes over with her eyes flashing excitement, "we have to tell Peter and the others."

Mary Magdalene shakes her head. "You go. I want to stay here." She feels a tug on her sleeve and turns to face Joanna.

"It's not safe. The soldiers could come."

"Let them!" Mary Magdalene says softly. Joanna takes her hand.

"Joanna, we have to hurry!" Salome cries. Joanna looks beseechingly at Mary Magdalene.

"Please," Mary Magdalene answers. "I want to pray." Joanna kisses her and hurries off with Salome.

Mary Magdalene reenters the tomb and sits on the stone bench where they had laid him. Picking up the winding cloths, she clasps them to her. *My prayers have been answered. He has risen as he said he would. What will life be like now? Will he walk with us again? Perform his miracles? Will the Romans hunt him? Hunt us? He said he would come back, but he never told us where to meet him or what we would be doing.* Then she remembered him saying he would send the Holy Spirit. *Was the angel the Holy Spirit? So many questions and I am still so alone. Please God, bring him back to us.* Then the silence of the tomb is broken by her plaintive cry.

"I don't want to live without him."

*T*HE CRY ECHOED across the landscape as the two badly frightened young soldiers crouch on the ground under the trees. Claudius grabs his companion, Lucius.

"Did you hear that?" he asks.

Lucius nods.

"I won't go back there!" Rubbing his eyes, Claudius says, "By Apollo—I didn't think I'd ever see again."

"What will we tell them?" Lucius asks, concerned.

"That the Galileans came, overpowered us, and stole the body."

"You're mad! They'll have us beaten. Why don't we tell them the truth?"

"Which is?"

Lucius stands up and looks down at him. "Jupiter came down from heaven, shaking the earth, and rolled the stone aside. Then Juno herself appeared in all her radiance, blinding us and knocking us to earth."

Claudius is totally shocked by this suggestion. "You *really* believe that?"

Lucius nods. Claudius is doubtful.

"But will they?"

PETER'S THOUGHTS ARE a jumble as he races toward the tomb. *An angel. They saw an angel. Did they make this up? Salome might; she's always trying to make herself more important, but Joanna wouldn't. If she says she saw an angel, then you can bet she did. Mary, Jesus' mother, saw an angel when she conceived. Joseph, his father, said he did, too. But an angel that said Jesus has risen? If he has risen, where is he?* He picks up his pace as John passes him. As he reaches the tomb, Peter is glad to see that John has waited for him to go in first.

Inside he sees Mary Magdalene sitting quietly, the linen cloths and head wrap rolled up on her lap.

Stunned, he mutters, "He's gone." John joins them as Mary nods her head.

"He told us he would rise." Her voice is calm

Peter feels John's touch on his shoulder. "They'll say we've taken him!"

Peter turns to him. "We'll be hunted men. We must leave Jerusalem."

The two men turn to go.

*M*ARY SAYS IN a low voice, "I'm staying."

She watches as Peter turns and looks back at her. *Poor Peter—I can practically see the workings of his brain, feverishly processing the odds. Flee or stay? Survive or save face?* She feels a sudden rush of compassion for him. *So much of himself is invested in what others think of him, as though he can only see himself through their eyes. How he must miss seeing himself through Jesus' eyes in a moment like this….*

"Fine! John and I will lay low," Peter answers and then turns to John. "Let's move the stone back. No one will ever know."

Mary Magdalene says firmly, "No! Everyone needs to know that it happened as he said it would."

Mary watches Peter, puzzled by the deeply pained look on his face. Her heart goes out to him as he turns with his shoulders slumped underneath a heavy unspoken weight.

As the men run off, Mary Magdalene stands at the opening, stretching out both arms to grasp the sides of the tomb, and drops her head in reflection. *I'll stay here until he comes. He will come; I know he will.* The stillness of the morning is broken by bird chirps. She listens to their cacophony, and then hearing movement, she raises her head and sees a hooded figure clothed in rough garments coming up the path.

As Mary tentatively moves toward the figure, she can't quite make out who it is, but she feels a stirring of excitement. *Could it be he?* The figure stops a short distance away.

"Mary."

Recognizing Jesus' voice, Mary Magdalene begins to run toward him.

"Teacher!" She reaches out to embrace him.

Jesus steps back and says tenderly and beseechingly, "Don't cling to me, Mary."

Feeling rebuffed, she steps back, lowers her head, and says with all the pain in her, "I thought my heart would break."

"It was my Father's will."

"I don't understand."

"I did what I did out of love."

"Love for... us?"

"Love for all."

Mary Magdalene struggles to understand. "Your sufferings showed us what love is."

"I will go to the Father soon. Tell my brothers and sisters you've seen me."

She begins to cry. "Please take me with you."

"You have work to do here, Mary. Teach others as I have taught you. The work won't be easy, but remember I am always with you."

Jesus disappears abruptly. Mary Magdalene looks up, expecting him to linger skyward. Then she examines the ground for his footprints. Nothing—he's gone, leaving no trace. She falls to the ground and lies on the cold earth. *He walks among us as he said he would. He loves me still, but this task he has set for me—to tell the others. The women will be overjoyed, but the men … they'll be doubtful and distrusting. Peter especially will not welcome such news from me.* She remembers all the incidents in the past when she and Peter had clashed. *He's jealous of me. He'll think I made this up to raise myself up over him. I don't have the strength for this.*

She goes back to the comfort and safety of the tomb. *I'll stay here and pray,* she thinks. *No one needs to know. This will be my secret.* The thought fills her with comfort. *He is here. He is mine. Mine.*

But he said, "Love for all." I was hoping to hear him say just this once that he loved me and that I was special to him. I know I was. I saw it in his eyes, in the way he looked at me. Me. But he also looked that way at John, his favorite among the men. He put his arms around John as he did all the men but never the women—except, on occasion, his mother. No, he reserved radiant smiles for us women as thanks for our labor and what we brought to him. It enabled all of us to live, but I never felt his full embrace.

But he appeared to me. He asked me to spread the good news—to tell all the others.

What a fool I am. Of course, I'm special to him. I'm sitting here like a foolish, romantic girl and I'm not accepting his real gift to me. He came to me.

Oh Lord, I am not worthy that you should have come to me! The words of the centurion whose servant he cured came to her, "Oh Lord, I am not worthy that you should come under my roof. Say but the word and my servant shall be healed." *Oh Lord, say but the word and my soul shall be healed!*

How has he done it? It's another miracle like all the others. Only this time, instead of Lazarus, he has brought himself back from the dead. How does he have the power to do that? The others he had healed through God's power. Has God raised him? Or has he raised himself? Is he then God? No, that is blasphemy. There can only be one God, and he shall never have false gods before him. Then who is Jesus? He says he is the Son of God…He certainly is a man, who laughed and cried and, yes, loved…Is he also God?

I mustn't think about this. It is enough that he has come to me. Will he come again?

Suddenly she hears the sound of loud voices speaking in a foreign tongue—Latin. Soldiers! She slips out of the tomb, runs, and hides in the heavy brush, watching as the soldiers approach and discover that the stone has been rolled back. She sees them disappear into the cavernous space. She waits and then hears their shouts from within the tomb.

"His followers stole the body!"

"Pilate must hear of this!"

Mary Magdalene feels no fear, only the love and peace that is flooding her. She lies back in the tall grass and begins to smell the heavy fragrances of the meadow's flowers. The aroma is so heady she feels as if she has never before smelled a flower. Her head swims with the sheer delight of what is enveloping her, and she luxuriates in these new feelings.

Soon she hears that all is quiet. *The soldiers must have left,* she guesses. She realizes that a lot more is at stake than her relationship with Peter. *They will begin hunting the men down as Peter predicted. I need to act and do what Jesus has asked of me.*

She shakes herself out of her newfound euphoria and runs excitedly toward Joanna's house.

Chapter Three

KNEELING BESIDE SALOME, Joanna tries to pray but concern for Mary Magdalene keeps nagging at her. She fears that the soldiers have come and arrested her. *What will they do to her, with the body gone? Will they punish her for telling the truth?*

Joanna looks over at Mary, who is still lying on the mat and very ill now with a fever that has kept climbing. Joanna suspects the older woman's mind can't let go of that last horrific image: her precious son hanging on a cross with his face contorted in pain. Joanna watches as she twists and turns, caught in this spiral of fevered anxiety. *I don't know what we can do to give her some relief. Something has to happen and soon or ....*

JUST THEN MARY Magdalene enters, breathless but looking radiant. "I saw Jesus. He's alive! He spoke to me!"

Mary Magdalene pauses, awaiting their reactions. The stunned women stare. Mary sits up. Mary Magdalene goes and kneels beside her.

"Mother, he has risen!"

Mary whispers weakly. "He said he would."

Mary Magdalene kisses her lovingly and then rises to embrace Joanna and Salome. She watches as tears of gladness run down their faces.

"Hosanna!" Joanna cries.

Salome responds, "Praise Heaven!"

Joanna takes Mary Magdalene's arms. "Did he say anything?"

"He said he loves us, all of us!" She beams, watching the women smile and nod to one another. Then hesitantly she adds, "He asked me to tell the men."

"So go tell them," Salome retorts.

"I don't know if they'll believe me."

"Why shouldn't they?"

Mary Magdalene sees Joanna shoot her an understanding look. "Mary Magdalene is right. You know how some of them look at her when she's with the Lord."

"Men don't like women to know more than they do," Mary Magdalene adds, "but perhaps they'll believe if it comes from all of us."

She sees Salome grab her cloak. "I'll go with you."

Mary Magdalene turns to Joanna, who shakes her head. "I

can't. I need to go to Herod's to tell Chuza."

Yes, thinks Mary Magdalene, *Joanna is willing to miss the scene ahead. She's not needed now, so she'll go back to her beloved Chuza.* She turns and sees Salome getting ready.

Mary Magdalene watches Jesus' mother look up at the ceiling, and smile. She goes over to her. All her pain has seemingly disappeared.

"He walks the earth," she whispers to Mary Magdalene, "the miracle of it! I feel like I did in that moment when the angel appeared to me and told me I had won God's favor and would bear a son who would be great and would be called Son of the Most High."

Mary Magdalene feels someone kneel next to them. She turns to see Joanna, cloaked, lean toward Mary and kiss her on the forehead.

"May I leave you for an hour? Chuza should be done with Herod's morning business by now."

Mary smiles at both women and nods. Holding back joyful tears, Mary Magdalene and Joanna get up and head for the door, where they are joined by Salome.

*J*OANNA HEADS FOR the splendid palace of the Hasmoneans, Herod Antipas's residence when in Jerusalem. Joanna knows the beautiful building with its complex architecture, large courts, and lavish baths well. She also knows it is valued chiefly because it affords a splendid view of the Temple Mount, where Herod Antipas can lie in his dining room, eat, and watch the comings and goings in the temple—something that mightily annoys the priests.

As a child, Joanna had spent much of her life in great palaces. Her mother had been a lady-in-waiting to Herod Antipas's mother, and they had stayed in the magnificent palace of Herod the Great—currently the home of Pontius Pilate—when the court had been in Jerusalem. But most of the time Joanna and her mother had stayed in Herod's palace in Jericho, the finest of them all. How she had enjoyed the terraced gardens with its fountains and waterfalls. Most of all she had loved the swimming pool. That had been where she had first met Chuza, her beloved husband, then a child like herself. He was the son of Herod the Great's steward. Her mother had tried to separate them, but they had always found a way to meet, and after her mother's death, they had married.

Chuza is now the steward himself, working for Herod Antipas, the son of Herod the Great and tetrarch of Galilee and Perea. After the death of Herod the Great, the kingdom was divided in thirds. Herod Antipas's brother Archelaus, son of the Samaritan Malthace, received the center of the country—Idumaea, Judea, and Samaria. His brother Philip inherited the region beyond Lake Gennesareth. Whatever their titles, the real power rested elsewhere—with Rome!

$\mathcal{T}$HIS MORNING CHUZA, a large, handsome man in his late thirties, stands in front of an imposing desk, the focal point of a sumptuously appointed room in the palace. He is discussing issues with his master, Herod, a lumbering man of fifty-three with dyed black hair, who is seated there.

"Do you have any other business for me, Chuza?"

"Just one thing, Excellency. That Hiram from the country?"

"Yes?"

"His loads have been light and haven't matched his bills."

"Document it."

"I have. If it continues, I'll replace him."

"Good."

"My Lord," says Chuza, bowing his head briefly in salute. Chuza turns to leave. He reaches the door—

"Chuza! One more thing." Chuza turns and walks back.

"My Lord?"

"That Jesus they're all talking about, the one who was crucified? He seemed to recognize you when he was before me."

"Yes."

"You knew him?"

"I saw him in passing."

"Are you a follower?"

"Of course not!"

"Good. You know I expect my steward to be vigilant in my interests." Chuza hears his tone darken menacingly. *"Mine and mine alone."*

Chuza grimly nods, indicating he understands.

*S*USANNA, HER FACE still pale from the trauma of watching Jesus' death, sits at a carved table in a luxurious room with a magnificent Persian rug; tall, intricately painted vases from Greece; and large windows overlooking a flower garden. Images from that horrendous day clamor for space in her mind: the crown of thorns piercing his head, blood running in rivulets down his face, the whip lacerating his back. She pushes them away to address the task at hand, writing her accounts on a tablet. She is housing and feeding twenty people in addition to her staff.

She remembers the years after her husband's death that she spent on the road with Jesus, along with Mary, Mary Magdalene, the apostles, and the other men and women who were his disciples. *How I treasure those memories. How carefree we all were, with our hearts singing with love for him and for each other.*

But there had been little money other than what Mary Magdalene, Joanna, and I had provided. Ah, Joanna. When she had joined them, Joanna had brought reassurance, emotional support, and, yes, financial security, the precious commodity that had kept this great mission going. There had been as many needs then as now—food and drink, of course; new clothes and sandals; herbs for the sick. The list had kept growing.

A knock at the door provides welcome relief from her conflicting thoughts. She looks up as Silas, her steward, enters the room.

"The crowd from Bethany is here—with baggage," announced the tall, lean red-headed man.

"Well, show them in!"

She notices his eyes flash, making his face look fox-like. His answer barely masks his hostility. "Where will we put them, Mistress?"

She looks at him coldly. "Clear out one of the lower rooms for Mary and Martha. Lazarus can stay with the men."

"Three more mouths to feed," Silas sneers.

"Hospitality comes first."

Susanna notes Silas's irritation as he ushers in the distraught Mary, Martha, and Lazarus of Bethany. Her attention turns to her guests.

Angular and thin, the sisters resemble one another. Their older brother, Lazarus, a man of medium height and build in his early thirties, is normally a placid-looking man, but today his face is etched with pain.

"We came as soon as we heard," Mary says.

Susanna watches as Mary and Martha begin to cry. She gathers them in her capacious arms. "Come. The others are already here."

*I*N THE UPPER room, Peter and John, still in the throes of grief, pack their belongings. As he grabs the last few items and shoves them in his bag, Peter can't shake the awful fear that Jesus would see him as running away and not facing up to what needs to be done in Jerusalem. *But I must go. I've had enough of soldiers with their lances, whips, and threats. I am a coward, and I don't have the stomach for this. How I long for my boat, my nets, the fresh smell of* *the sea filling my lungs, and the wind whipping through my hair.*

He waits impatiently as Susanna and Martha of Bethany collect the porridge bowls from breakfast. Seeing Miriam, who doesn't want to leave, crying softly in the arms of Mary of Bethany, he thinks, *Cleopas is going to have his hands full with her.*

Peter notices that the other apostles are ready for the journey and waiting patiently. Then he sees Andrew, who stands apart from the others and looks at him. Peter thinks he reads contempt on Andrew's face.

"Andrew, what are you waiting for?" he cries out to him angrily. "Get your things together!"

"No, Peter, I won't. We can't slink away like whipped dogs. Jesus came to Jerusalem to preach his word. We need to spread his message. We must stay."

"You stay; the rest of us are leaving."

Thomas exclaims, "Andrew, it's the only sane thing to do!" Peter shoots a grateful look at Thomas then notices that Cleopas is about to weigh in.

"Miriam and I are not waiting any longer. We're heading for Nain tomorrow."

Hearing a knock on the door, Peter gestures for silence. Matthew opens the door and gives Peter a relieved look when he sees Mary Magdalene and Salome. Mathew motions for them to come in.

"Peace be with you," Mary Magdalene greets the men reservedly.

Peter immediately tenses at the sight of her. He knows she will make this harder, and he wishes they had already been off before she had come. He watches Salome go directly to her son, James the Elder, and asks how he is.

"Ashamed," he replies. "You stayed with him, and I ran away."

Peter stiffens as he overhears James's answer. He watches Salome embrace her son, saying, "He knows you love him."

His focus shifts to Mary Magdalene, who has turned to the men. "I have good news." Peter and Matthew rise expectantly with her words. "I've seen the Lord."

Peter looks at her with naked hostility. *Why is she lying? What is she up to? Trying to keep us here? Trying to run the show, that's what she's doing!*

He is about to utter his thoughts when Thomas strides toward Mary Magdalene and shouts, "Impossible!" Andrew shoots Thomas a look.

"He appeared to me by the tomb," she replies.

Andrew asks, "Did he say anything?"

"He asked me to tell you that he'll be returning to his Father."

Peter looks at her in disbelief and then turns to the other men. "Why would he speak to her rather than to us?"

Peter notices Thomas, who is glaring at Mary. "He didn't speak to anyone!" he insists, "He's dead."

"Why don't you believe me? He spoke to me. He walks the earth. Peter, it happened and he is with us." Mary says beseechingly.

Peter turns to the men with a bitter look exclaiming, "Behold—the mouthpiece of Jesus!"

"Peter!" Peter turns to face his brother, Andrew, and sees the anger on his face.

Andrew bursts out, "Control your temper!"

Peter bristles as Matthew approaches him, saying, "You're turning against Mary as if she wasn't one of us."

Peter shouts at him, "You expect me to follow a woman now?"

"No, Peter," Mary Magdalene stares right at Peter and retorts, "I expect you to follow Jesus." Peter looks away.

"Peter," Salome bursts out, "haven't we women been with you from the beginning?"

"Didn't we travel with you?" Mary Magdalene responds.

Peter sees Susanna come closer and look at him with uncomprehending eyes. "Haven't we opened our homes to you?"

"Aren't we your sisters in Jesus?" Mary Magdalene continues and Peter hears the sadness in her voice.

He turns and sees Mary, Martha, and Lazarus of Bethany huddled together as though they are unable to understand how this group that had been so cohesive in Jesus' presence could be so at odds. Mary of Bethany looks up at Peter and catches his gaze.

"Aren't we all his followers?" she says.

Mary Magdalene adds emphatically, "Jesus made no distinction between a man and a woman."

Peter feels overwhelmed with conflicting emotions—he knows

in his heart the truth, but his pride has been wounded unfairly in his eyes. *They're ganging up on me. What's my authority worth anyway? It's all her fault. That Magdalene. She's always interfering and making my life difficult.* He swallows and sulks.

"I spoke hastily," he growls unrepentantly.

Peter watches Matthew try to bring the group back together. "Let's all rejoice that Jesus has risen from the dead." He heads to the corner and turns away. He can feel the tone of the room shift as everyone comes together.

He hears Mary Magdalene answer, "Praise be to God."

John's voice echoes throughout the room, "Hosanna in the Highest."

Peter feels the weight sink deeper in his chest.

*C*HUZA IS DISTRACTED as he checks a wagonload of food with one of his employees. He can't get his mind off the scene with Herod. *He knows or is he just guessing? How much does he really know? Is he aware that Joanna followed Jesus, traveled with him, and provided money for his needs?* He notices his employee looking at him quizzically as he counts the same goods over and over and Joshua, the merchant, staring at him anxiously each time he starts the count over.

Chuza, pulling himself together, warns him, "Looks a little light again, Joshua."

"I promise you, Chuza, I checked it myself."

"Check it again."

Just then, Chuza spots Joanna as she enters the gate. He sees her nods discreetly at him and then enters their house, the largest and closest to the palace of the Hasmoneans. Beside it are several other houses of varying size for the servants and a large barn for the chariots and animals.

Chuza, worried about what news she brings, hands his notes to his employee. "Continue. I'll be back."

He follows Joanna into the house, which is palatial in comparison to his mother's house inside Jerusalem. The ceilings are high and detailed, the pillows are covered in luxurious fabrics, and the furniture is ornate. Chuza goes directly to Joanna, who is waiting for him in the hall.

"I've been so concerned for you," he says as he tries to kiss her.

As she averts her face, he pulls aside her headscarf and buries his face in her hair. Just her familiar smell intoxicates him and makes him forget his concerns momentarily. He feels Joanna gently pull back.

"Jesus has risen! Mary Magdalene saw him."

The news hits Chuza like a blow. Stunned and worried, he moves away. "If this gets out, it will be an even greater threat to the priests and to Herod."

Joanna shakes her head, not understanding, "Threat?"

"I was there when Jesus was brought before Herod. Caiaphas and Annas accused Jesus of blasphemy for saying that he would sit on the right hand of God."

"Is that why they crucified him?"

"That and the fact that the zealots wanted someone as a rallying point."

"But Jesus would never lead a revolution."

"They could have used him. He rode into Jerusalem from Bethany, gathering more and more people as he went. They believed he was the Messiah."

"But Jesus preached peace, not war."

"Do you think the Romans weren't watching him? And the high priests? Joanna, open your eyes. What was the first thing he did in Jerusalem? He went into the temple and drove out those who were buying and selling. Who owns all those businesses?" His words cause Joanna to shake her head in mystification. "Annas and Caiaphas do. The cattle market, the doves, even the hides after the beasts have been killed—everything that is used for sacrifice—is controlled by those two men with the blessing of Rome. Annas is a Roman appointee, and for the last thirty years he and his family have been in Rome's pocket and have profited mightily from it."

He watches Joanna sinks to the floor in shock. "They are supposed to be holy men."

"That is what Jesus meant when he said, 'God's house is a house of prayer; you have made it a den of thieves.' Do you think the priests took that lightly?"

He sees that Joanna understands now. "Jesus came to purify the temple."

Chuza continues his argument. "And when he raised Lazarus from the dead in Bethany, he was only two miles away. Word of it streaked through Jerusalem like lightning, frightening the high priests. It was a great affront to their power."

Joanna replies, "That was a miracle!"

"Yes, and who raises men from the dead but God himself?"

"Chuza, we need to tell people about Jesus' resurrection to help them to believe."

The blood drains from his face as he realizes how naïve she is and how unaware of the danger facing them. *I must protect her.* Taking her in his arms, he murmurs. "I believed. I still believe." Putting his hand to her breast, he tells her, "I knew he was more than a prophet when he healed that growth in your breast. I love you, Joanna."

"And I love you. You're an extraordinary man—to have let me go to Jesus and follow him."

"But now you must be cautious." He watches Joanna's face look at him with alarm. "They could decide to raid Susanna's house and arrest everyone. You mustn't go there for a while."

"We should both go there. We're part of them, Chuza, and Susanna counts on us."

"Mary Magdalene can take the money to her."

"But how will I explain this to the other women?"

"Tell them I want my wife here with me."

He sees the stricken look on his wife's face, and he knows she never anticipated this outcome.

ANNAS SHIFTS FROM one foot to the other in the cool morning air, watching the steam from his breath rise and feeling his beard damp with dew. *Why should I, who once was the high priest, have to be here in this ungodly hour when my bones are aching from the cold? It's Pilate's fault. He sent two schoolboys to protect the tomb.* Annas rages inwardly at yet another example of what he considers is Pilate's contempt.

He looks without an ounce of pity at the two young Roman soldiers, their backs bared and bloody as they hang against the pillars in the center of the stone prison courtyard. Annas turns to the reigning high priest, Caiaphas, his son-in-law, also watching the interrogation.

"We've got to get something out of them. They're making us look like fools."

Caiaphas nods and signals the high-ranking soldier with the whip. On Caiaphas' order, the whips slashes another time.

"Are you ready to change your story?" he commands.

No response. He whips them each some more. Both men sob with the pain.

Caiaphas snarls, "His followers took him, didn't they?"

"No! No! There was a violent earthquake," the first soldier answers.

As the whip hits his back, the second one cries out, "Someone appeared who shone like lightning."

Annas looks at Caiaphas and sees the frustration on his face. He watches as Caiaphas walks behind the pillar and looks the foot soldier in the face.

"You're lying! What did they pay you to tell this story?"

No response. The priest turns to the soldier with the whip. "Continue. Kill them with the whip if they won't talk." Caiaphas walks back to Annas, "We're not getting anywhere with those two. We need to identify the women who anointed the body."

Annas' eyes narrow. "Perhaps we should send for Saul of Tarsus."

Caiaphas flashes a broad smile. "Yes, he's done a good job of smoking out Jewish dissidents in other places. He would make short work of these blasphemers."

Chapter Four

*M*IRIAM FEELS THE baby kick with every step the ass takes. She looks back at Jerusalem fading in the distance. *I am so happy there among people who love me. How I will miss them and miss being a part of something so much bigger than Cleopas and me. Life in Nain will be so much quieter.*

Suddenly Miriam feels the weight of exhaustion, and she doubles over the donkey's back. She glances up to see Cleopas, who is leading the beast, look back at her lovingly and then alarmingly. He stops the donkey, moves to her side, lifts her off, and puts his arm around her.

Miriam says gratefully, "Thanks. I'm still tired, I guess."

"I'm sorry to push you, but my father will be furious that we've been gone so long. He'll know we've followed Jesus again."

She answers wearily, "We'll just have to bear his wrath." She smiles at the tender look Cleopas gives her.

"You are so brave!" he exclaims. "You were so brave to follow Jesus to Golgotha—and so foolish."

She places her hand on his arm, looking up at him, "I've loved him since that incredible day when he raised your cousin from the dead."

She feels Cleopas take her in his arms and kiss her, the memory of Jesus and his vibrant charisma strengthening their love. Cleopas breaks the spell.

"I don't want to, but we should be going if we're to get to Emmaus before nightfall. Do you want to get back on the donkey?"

"I'd rather walk for a while."

She looks up and sees a stranger coming toward them, wearing a large turban-like hat and carrying a walking stick. *There is something so familiar about him. Where might I have seen him before?* He falls into step with them.

"You seem very sad," he says.

Cleopas answers, "Are you the only one in Jerusalem who hasn't heard what's happened during the last few days?"

"What?"

"Jesus the Nazarene, a great prophet and healer, was crucified. We were hoping that it was he who was going to deliver Israel."

"Are you a zealot?"

Cleopas shakes his head vehemently. "No sir—a pacifist like my Lord. He rode into Jerusalem last week on a donkey...," motioning to theirs, "not a warhorse like the Romans."

The stranger replies, "The prophet Zachariah said that a humble king would come riding a donkey."

Miriam smiles as she listens to Cleopas answer excitedly, "But he was so much more than a king. He brought the dead to life."

The stranger answers, "You make this Jesus of yours sound as though he had the power of God."

Cleopas responds to the stranger's conclusion. "He did! There's an inn coming up. Will you dine with us?"

"You honor me."

At this, Miriam beams with pleasure; she's so proud of her husband's easy way with a guest.

CLEOPAS FEELS PROUD as the innkeeper leads them through the dark, dank-smelling inn crowded with the last of the Passover pilgrims. He knows this dinner will bring him perilously close to an empty purse, but it's worth it to have the opportunity to host this elegant man and introduce him to Jesus. He tells the innkeeper that they would like a place where they can speak privately and is grateful when they are seated in a quiet corner on large pillows. Cleopas urges his guest to sit in the center between Miriam and him.

Speaking in a low voice, he tells the stranger, "Jesus performed many miracles. At the wedding of my cousins in Cana, they ran out of wine. Jesus turned water into wine, so they wouldn't be shamed before their guests.

The stranger smiled broadly on hearing this. Cleopas, so involved with his story, didn't seem to notice.

"Another time," Cleopas continued, "he made a few loaves and some fish enough to feed thousands of people."

Smiling again the stranger observed, "Your Master seemed very concerned that people would have enough to eat and drink."

Before Cleopas could answer, he caught the look on Miriam's face. He knew she feared that their guest wouldn't understand the power of Jesus and smiled as she, bursting with excitement, speaks.

"Cleopas's own cousin Elijah was dead. He was being carried in a funeral procession. His mother, Ruth, was weeping inconsolably. Jesus, watching her, said to Elijah, 'Arise and walk!' Elijah lifted his head from the bearer's hands and sat up. Some women in the crowd fainted from astonishment. Men looked at him with disbelief! Tears ran down Aunt Ruth's cheeks from joy. Elijah leaped down and asked, 'Mother, why are you weeping? I am alive and well!'"

The stranger asks, "Was the young man's mother a widow?"

Miriam is startled that he would have guessed that. "Yes."

"Perhaps Jesus took pity on her fear that she would be alone in her old age."

Cleopas heard Miriam gasp at this man's understanding.

When the food is placed before them, the stranger removes his hat. Cleopas looks at him quizzically.

"Please, sir, serve yourself."

Cleopas sees the look on Miriam's face as she studies the stranger. He can tell by how focused she is that she feels like she knows him from someplace. *Why? He's just a stranger we met on the road.*

The man says, "Thank you, my God, for this bread, which we offer to you." He raises the bread and addresses the two. "This is my body which is given for you."

Miriam and Cleopas in amazement exchange glances. Cleopas thinks to himself, *Could it possibly be he?* The stranger gives a piece of bread to Miriam and then Cleopas, who eat it. He pours wine for each of them and raises his cup.

"This is my blood that was shed for you."

It is he! Cleopas looks at Miriam and now knows that they both realize it is Jesus who is seated with them. Cleopas sits stunned. Miriam can't contain her excitement.

"Lord!"

Jesus then vanishes from their sight.

Cleopas looks at Miriam and confirms, "That was our Jesus!"

"We're truly blessed!"

They fall into each other's arms with tears streaming down their faces at the realization of what they have seen.

"Cleopas, we must go back to tell the others."

"No, Miriam, my father forbade us to go. If I'm not back soon, he'll know I disobeyed and we're certain to lose our inheritance. I know my father!"

"The others need to know," she insists.

Cleopas sees the look on her face and knows her mind is set. "You're willing to risk losing everything?"

With a look of utter seriousness on her face, she nods. "Jesus said that if he asks something difficult of us, he'll give us what we need to do it."

As Cleopas draws her to himself, he thinks, *I'm the luckiest man in Israel. I have a wonderful wife, a baby due, and a Savior who loved me enough to come to me himself. I am so blessed.*

The road stretches ahead, winding back toward Jerusalem and bringing back the familiar sights that they had experienced on their way out of the city. It might have been just a few hours ago, but to Cleopas, it feels like another lifetime. Like Miriam, he is still reeling from the encounter with Jesus, but something else weighs on his mind.

He remembers the last time he and Miriam disobeyed his father. Hearing so much about Jesus, especially from Elijah and his mother, Ruth, Miriam also wanted to meet him. Truth be told, he himself had wanted to be in the company of the man he considered the greatest to have ever walked the earth.

They got word that Jesus was to preach near his cousin's house in Cana. Even though it was close to planting time, his father had given them permission to visit. Knowing how his father had felt, he had said nothing about Jesus. When they had returned, his father had been furious. They had stayed away too long, and he suspected that they had as his father had said "followed that man."

"I forbade you to follow him, and you deliberately disobeyed me."

Cleopas had defended himself, "Father, Jesus is more than a prophet."

"A prophet? He is Jesus of Nazareth, son of Mary and Joseph. I attended his *bar mitzvah.*"

Arguing, Cleopas had replied, "You're not recognizing all he has done."

"Done? Turning water into wine? He does magic tricks and then parades himself as the Messiah."

It had taken every bit of strength Cleopas had to continue the argument. His father had had a knack for turning any reality into another. He remembered feeling the weight of years of living with this man. He could feel like a giant, and in a flash his father could reduce him to a gnat.

Cleopas had taken a deep breath and reminded him that Jesus had raised his father's own nephew Elijah from the dead.

"My foolish sister Ruth only thought he was dead," he had retorted.

Angered, Cleopas had shouted, "I saw him with my own eyes. He had no breath in him. If Jesus had come into Nain an hour later, he would have been buried. You know that."

"This is what I know. I forbade you to follow him, and you disobeyed me. If you ever do this again, you will have to leave my house and never return. You and yours will be dead to me!"

Those words ring in Cleopas' ears. He knows his father is a man of his word, and after this he will never take him back. He prays that Miriam is right and that Jesus will give him the strength he needs to go on and make a living for his wife and child.

A YOUNG BOY stands like a soldier on guard in front of the house where the women are staying. His new clothes and sandals look improbable on him because he is emaciated and his skin is marked with pox.

Joanna is at the door talking to Mary Magdalene, who quickly takes in Joanna's distress, and the boy, who is waiting for her.

Joanna hands Mary money. "Please give this to Susanna." Then, pointing to the boy, "From now on I'll be sending him."

Mary Magdalene looks at her quizzically.

"A street urchin. We took him in."

Mary Magdalene, her voice filled with concern for Joanna, asks, "Why can't you come yourself?"

"Herod suspects that we're followers. I mustn't come anymore."

Mary Magdalene, feeling a stab of fear for her friend, shakes her head. "No!"

Joanna swallows hard. "Don't worry. I'll make sure you have everything you need."

The women embrace, holding each other close. Mary Magdalene sees the tears spring into Joanna's eyes. Mary Magdalene thinks, *How*

like Joanna to be threatened and yet to think of everyone but herself.
She whispers to her, "May Jesus be with you."

IN A SMALL room off of the main altar of the temple, Annas and Caiaphas remove and fold their ceremonial robes. They then move to a table on which are stacked large rolls of papyrus. As Caiaphas unrolls the top one, Annas looks anxiously to know the profits made from Passover.

"And how much did we make on the cattle this year?"

"Thirty thousand denarii."

"Their hides, plus those of the cattle brought into Jerusalem, will yield another ten thousand."

"And the doves?"

"Another ten thousand. Putting in the additional pools was a good idea. I don't have all the figures in yet for the charges for ritual cleansing, but we estimate that there were a half a million pilgrims this year."

"The moneychangers paid us in silver—more than twenty thousand pieces."

"Passover got off to a poor start with that crazy man wreaking havoc on their booths."

"Will his followers do more of the same?"

"This story of his so-called resurrection will embolden them."

They are both lost in thought, worried about this challenge to their authority. Annas looks at Caiaphas and waits for his reaction.

Finally Caiaphas speaks up. "What do you think the Jesus people are plotting?"

Annas answers grimly, "We need to find out. I'll send the guards to the house where they've gathered."

Annas notices that Caiaphas is smiling craftily.

"Don't. I have a better idea. I'll make sure one of ours is in there with them." He pauses and thinks of who that might be. "Silas. The redhead. He's dissatisfied."

"He's a good one, but that may not be enough."

"I know. I contacted Saul of Tarsus."

"Excellent! Let him find the women who anointed the body."

Chapter Five

*M*IRIAM IS KEYED up with the excitement of the news they will tell and relieved that this has brought them back to Jerusalem, to the center of things, where she wants to be. *Perhaps Susanna will offer us a room of our own, she thinks. It would be like having a little house. We would be surrounded by people who love us, and Mary could deliver the baby.*

Finally, she and Cleopas reach the courtyard of Susanna's place, a large walled compound with stables and a freestanding outdoor kitchen. Miriam watches as Susanna and a servant, Uriah, who is strong for such a slight man, lift a large pot of porridge on the fire for the next morning's breakfast. She sees Silas, the steward, come from the back of the house with an armful of wood and give them an apprizing look. They walk up to Susanna, who turns and lights up when she sees them.

"Welcome! We didn't think you would be back so soon!"

Cleopas helps Miriam off the ass. "It's good to be back here."

Miriam can't contain herself any longer. "We have news!"

She is about to continue when Susanna stops her and turns to Silas. Miriam notices that he has put the wood down to listen.

"Take care of the animal," Susanna admonishes him.

He smiles at her ingratiatingly. "Uriah can do that. I'll tend to your guests, Mistress."

Miriam watches him take the bags off the animal and starts toward the stairs with them. She notices the exasperated look on Susanna's face as she gives further instructions.

"Prepare one of the ground floor rooms for them, and that will be all."

Miriam sees Susanna gesture for them to follow her toward the outside steps. She briefly feels a twinge of worry about the robe hidden in one of the bags as she looks anxiously behind her at Silas. He seems to be steaming as he watches them walk away.

$\mathcal{M}$ARY MAGDALENE, STARTLED by seeing Miriam and Cleopas return, intuits what their news will be. *Of course,* she thinks, *he is walking the earth. Many will see him.* She gathers with Peter and the others around Cleopas and Miriam as James the Elder questions them.

"If it was our Lord, why didn't you know him right away?"

Mary Magdalene remembers, *I didn't recognize him at first either. I was so caught up in wanting to see him. I still long to see him again.* Her thoughts are interrupted by an explosion of anger from Thomas.

"You expect us to believe it was him?"

She flinches at the accusation in his words and feels herself shrinking back. *Why does he have to be so predictable with his doubt and hostility?* She looks at Miriam, whose face seems to show only empathy and sadness.

"Oh, Thomas," Miriam says quietly. Mary Magdalene looks back at Thomas. Her pity seems to energize him even more.

"I would have to put my fingers into the nail holes before I would believe!"

As he says this, there is a noise at the door, as if someone is trying to open it. They all go quiet. All eyes leap toward the door.

"The door is double bolted," Thomas whispers.

The noise at the door is louder now.

Thomas exclaims, "They've come for us!"

Suddenly, the door becomes a sheet of light, and then the whole wall lights up. Through it, Jesus appears. He now wears no disguise but looks as he did when he was alive. Mary sees that the men are stunned and shaken. She looks around joyously at them and whispers a silent, *Thank you, Lord.* She hears Mary call out to her son and sees her run to Jesus and embrace him.

"I knew I would see you again!"

Jesus kisses his mother tenderly and whispers, "Blessed Mother."

Mary Magdalene joyously proclaims, "Jesus!"

She hears Peter cry out, "Lord!"

Looking at all of them with great love, Jesus says, "Peace be with you."

Mary Magdalene sees that the apostles are afraid and shrink from him as he walks toward them. She can tell that Jesus is playful as he had been at the door, obviously enjoying their surprise.

Laughing, he says, "Why are you frightened? Touch me and make sure I'm not a ghost!" He turns to Thomas. "Thomas, put your finger here in my wrist and bring your hand to my side. Believe."

Mary Magdalene holds her breath as she watches Thomas' reaction. Thomas draws his hand back. "My Lord and my God."

Her eyes dart to Matthew and Philip, who seem to exchange alarmed glances on hearing Thomas' strong words. Mary Magdalene knows that their fellow Jews would regard the statement as blasphemous, and the Romans would consider them treasonous. As Mary Magdalene looks back at Jesus, she sees his concern is different as he looks at Thomas.

"You believe because you've seen me." Then he looks at all of them. "Blessed are those who haven't seen me and believe."

Mary smiles as she observes that the apostles are transfixed. Jesus turns to Susanna.

"Susanna, do you have anything here to eat?"

A meal of fish, honeycomb, and fruit is laid out on the table. Surrounded by the apostles, Jesus eats leisurely and with relish.

Mary Magdalene smiles as she observes him. *Only Jesus would think of taking time to eat at a moment like this.* She recalls their last supper together, the Sabbath banquet with Martha and Mary, and so many other meals they had shared with him. *Jesus seems to do a lot of his preaching around food. Maybe he understands that minds relax and open up when the body is sated. Maybe the food gives him the energy to feed the rest of them spiritually.* Not for the first time, she marvels at how in touch he is with his senses while simultaneously appearing to be outside of them. *How can such a God be the most human of men?*

Mary Magdalene watches Susanna bring Jesus bread. As he takes it, Mary observes the look of love that flits across Susanna's face. Susanna grasps his other hand and kisses it. He smiles down at her and thanks her tenderly.

After a moment, Jesus puts the bread down and turns serious. "You've seen the prophecies come true."

Mary Magdalene answers, "Yes, Lord."

Jesus smiles at Mary Magdalene and pats her hand. She beams at him and then notices Peter looking at her with dismay. *Oh yes, the old jealousy is still there.* Peter brushes past her to kneel at Jesus' side.

"Lord, it's wonderful to have you with us."

Peter cringes when Jesus says solemnly to him, "Yet you didn't believe I was among you until you saw me for yourself." Then Jesus addresses the group. "I came to you so that you would believe and tell all nations about me. I'm sending you as the Father sent me."

Mary Magdalene immediately answers, "We will go, Lord. We'll preach the message of love to others."

Mary Magdalene sees the annoyed glance Peter throws at her before he turns to Jesus and says sadly, "Who will follow me? I'm just a fisherman."

"Let souls be your catch."

"But, Master, I don't have the words. There are no parables in me."

Jesus reassures him. "The Holy Spirit will come to you." Then he turns to address all assembled, "You'll be filled with power from heaven."

She wonders, *What sort of power? Power like yours, Lord? But we'll know that in due time, won't we?* She turns to Jesus.

"When, Lord?"

"Stay here in the city and wait."

Then Mary Magdalene sees Jesus disappear by walking through the wall and hears the group gasp. She experiences a profound sense of loss as he once again leaves her. Miriam tugs at her sleeve and she knows Miriam is eager to discuss what has happened. She watches as the men huddle together, one outdoing the other in his commentary. She turns and gathers the lovely Miriam in her arms. As the women gaze into each other's eyes, they share a wordless moment of awe at what they have experienced.

$\mathcal{M}$IRIAM LOOKS THROUGH the branches of the olive tree to the sky above. Where does he go when he disappears? Up in the sky? Is that where his Father is? Or is he simply walking the earth as he had done on the afternoon we met him on the road to Nain? One thing she knows for sure is that he is in her heart, swelling it with gladness.

She bends back over the deep tub and picks out another garment. This one is heavy, one of Cleopas' robes. *Hard to get all the water out. I wonder if the branch will hold it.* She stretches her full length and then tosses the robe over the branch. *In a few months—maybe less—I will be washing the baby's things. Dear Jesus, let our baby be born easily. Let him be well.* Her mind drifts back to the evening before—the wonder of seeing him again and listening to his voice. She can contain her joy no longer and sings out in a robust voice.

"He has risen from the dead. Alleluia, alleluia.

"Risen as he truly said. Alleluia, alleluia."

Inside their room, which is lit only by two small slats high in the wall, she can hear Cleopas searching through their saddle bags.

"Where is my belt?" he calls out from inside.

"Alleluia, alleluia—," she continues until she realizes he is talking to her. "What did you say, love?"

No answer. Miriam shrugs as she hums a few more bars.

"Cleopas, I'm fifteen, married, with child..." She turns back to return to the room and stoops to enter the house. "And the Lord of all, the Master of the universe loves me. I am the richest..." Cleopas has Jesus' robe in his hands. "... girl in Israel."

Gruffly Cleopas asks, "What's this?"

"Jesus' seamless garment."

"Where did you get it?"

"The soldiers cast lots for it. I bought it from the one who won."

"Should you have this?"

"His mother wove it for him. I meant to give it to her, but there never seemed to be a right time."

She takes it from him and clutches it to her belly. She looks up at his perplexed face.

"Please, Cleopas, let me keep it for now." She looks back down. "It won't be long." She pauses. "Remember, my mother died giving birth to me."

Miriam looks up at Cleopas, whose face is consumed with worry.

*D*AWN BREAKS THE next morning, but dark clouds move across the plain on the road leading to Jerusalem. A rumble of thunder echoes over the landscape. As it fades out, the sound is replaced by the rhythmic stamping of hooves—an ominous drum roll coming from over the horizon. Two shepherds hurriedly move their sheep to the side of this stretch of newly constructed Roman road.

Suddenly the galloping legs of a horse appear, raising dust at breakneck speed. A tall, rangy man is riding a beautiful stallion hard.

Saul of Tarsus has arrived.

He overtakes a large caravan of camels laden with the goods of Damascus. He doesn't even notice the look of annoyance the merchants on their high perches give him. He doesn't see their drivers frantically move the camels so that the goods piled high on them won't plunge to the ground because of his impatience.

Saul's mind is elsewhere filled with zeal, confident in the righteousness of his cause. As he gazes at the hills of Jerusalem rising before him, he thinks of the line of the psalm, *"As the hills stand about Jerusalem, even so stands the Lord about his people, from this time forth and forevermore."*

Little does he know that he is the instrument sent to fulfill Jesus' prophecy: "Indeed the hour is coming when anyone who kills you will think he is doing a holy duty for God."

Chapter Six

*S*ITTING AT THE table with Susanna, Mary Magdalene can't help but see the look of worry on her friend's face. Noticing that some of the luxurious items in the comfortable, spacious office are now gone, she can guess the source of her friend's anxiety. But she has pressing worries of her own. She can't shake the feeling that Silas, Susanna's steward, seems to be keeping tabs on them. She finally resolves to say something.

"Silas seems to be everywhere. I keep running into him."

She looks at Susanna, who dismisses her concerns, and Mary Magdalene can tell Susanna's mind is clearly elsewhere.

"There's so much work to do. More people are added every day." She looks at Mary Magdalene. "I need more money."

"Joanna and Chuza will continue sending their contributions."

"Yes, but all these years—this one and the three before on the road—have drained my savings."

Mary Magdalene sees the worry and nods understandingly. "I still get money from Magdala, so you can count on me for more. I'll also ask the wealthier among us if they can contribute."

She covers Susanna's hand with hers. Susanna pulls away and shakes her head.

"But after last night, there may be many more followers."

"You're right. We could attract attention."

"I'm fortunate; I have a protector." Mary Magdalene looks at her questioningly. "A priest. A friend of my late husband's."

"I have a protector, too—Jesus—but we're going to have to start protecting ourselves. Let's keep an eye on Silas. I don't trust him."

*H*IS EYES ALWAYS have been his best weapon. When he stared into a guilty man's eyes, Saul of Tarsus had the ability to make his prisoner believe he could see into the culprit's soul. His mind is cunning, yes. His ways can be brutal. But he knows his eyes—cold, disdainful, and surgical—could fill grown men with irrational fear.

And the two pathetic specimens before him right now at the Gate of the Gardens aren't far from trembling themselves. These two Roman soldiers apparently had interacted with the women who had passed through with burial oils for Jesus. One is young and nervous. The other one is a petty bully, and Saul had broken tougher hides than his. But for the moment, he is just content to fix *the stare* on them and ask questions.

"Can you describe these women?"

The brute answers, "One of them thought she was a queen. I took her down a peg."

Saul notices that the younger one gives his smug compatriot a disgusted look. "You need to keep your hands to yourself."

The larger man laughs. "Don't forget these are Jews,"

Saul knows this idiot thinks he himself is a Roman because Tarsus is a Roman province and Jews don't ordinarily associate with Romans.

"How do you treat Jews in Tarsus?" the soldier asks with a wink.

Saul smiles and moves closer until he's inches away from the man's face, forcing him to blink. "We don't have your problem in Tarsus," he softly replies. He turns and addresses the other man. "Who else was there besides her?"

"There was an old woman missing several teeth and a tall woman, looked to be in her mid-thirties, who was dressed like a lady."

"Did they use names?"

"No. They were in a hurry to get to the tomb."

Saul thanks them, gives the larger oaf a long look, mounts his stallion, and rides off.

LATER THAT DAY Saul is leaving Annas' palace after a meeting with the two high priests. As he hurries through the great doors, he spots Gamaliel, the man he admires most in the world and his spiritual father, to whom he was sent to be educated.

He remembers that at age ten he had sailed from Tarsus to Caesarea. Accompanied by other pilgrims bound for the Holy Land, he had traveled over land to Jerusalem through a succession of hills and valleys and past terraced vineyards. With laughter, music, and song, their hearts filled with longing for the ancestral city, the pilgrims had surged forward until finally they had seen the city wall and the temple's glittering roof.

What a thrill it had been for him to pass through the city's gate and to finally be in Jerusalem—in spite of the tall, menacing Roman soldiers with swords ready to be pulled from their scabbards at a moment's notice. Their presence had been all the more reason for a young Jewish boy to long for the education that he had known he would find here. He was bound for the school of Hillel and its most eminent teacher, Gamaliel.

Saul pulls his mind from the past and refocuses on the present. His heart leaps as he comes closer to the white-bearded priest ascending the stairs below him to the broad landing.

"Teacher!" he cries and rushes to embrace him.

Gamaliel turns and Saul sees the surprise on his face. "What are you doing here, Saul? I thought you were in Damascus."

"Caiaphas sent for me." Gamaliel looks at him quizzically, and Saul laughs. "I'm to rid Jerusalem of the Jesus followers!" Saul is surprised by the horrified look on Gamaliel's face.

"No! Leave them alone."

"Rabbi, we're in an uneasy balance with the Romans. These false Jews imperil us."

"If this movement of theirs is of human origin, it will break up of its own accord."

Saul looks troubled. "And if it's not?"

Gamaliel warns, "You might find yourself fighting against God."

Saul is stunned as he watches Gamaliel continue up the stairs. He feels rejected and misunderstood by the man he reveres above all others as a man of much wisdom and learning. Rabbis came from the entire world to sit at his feet. The words of the prayer Gamaliel had taught him echoed in his head. *"Let there be no hope to them who apostatize from the true religion; and let heretics, how many so ever they be, all perish in a moment." These are the words that rule my life and that determine my course to weed out the apostates whoever and wherever they are. This is why I have been called to Jerusalem. What has changed in Gamaliel?*

*I*T'S EARLY EVENING outside Susanna's house. The sky darkens, and the candles have been lit inside. On the road leading to the house, a scarred male slave pulls a heavy cart. His master occasionally lashes at him with a whip.

"Faster! Do you want to make me miss my dinner?"

*I*NSIDE THE UPPER room in Susanna's house, the evening meal is finished and the women are gathering the dishes. Peter is at the window, distracted by the scene below. He shakes his head angrily, thinking *What a selfish fool.*

*M*ARY MAGDALENE PICKS up the plates of the men around Peter and banters with them.

"You women feed us well, Mary," John says.

Smiling, she answers, "We're all going to need our strength. We have a lot of work ahead of us."

As she reaches for Peter's plate, he abruptly rises. She loses her balance, and the metal plates fall to the floor with a clatter. She kneels to pick them up.

"You have a lot to say, Mary," Peter snips. She can hear the hostility in his voice.

Speaking from the kneeling position, she answers, "Does my speaking annoy you?"

Peter barks, "You annoy me!"

Mary reaches for another plate. "As you see, I am your servant."

Looking down at her, Peter answers, "And *that* is all you are."

Mary Magdalene rises and faces him. "And are you the slave of all?"

Peter asks, "Slave?"

"Jesus said that anyone who wishes to be first must be the slave of all."

With that, Mary Magdalene walks to the back of the room with the plates. She can tell that Peter is simmering because he gets up and paces.

"Now I'm to be a slave!"

Mary Magdalene sees John go over to him and try to quiet him.

"Mary has a place here. Use her, Peter. Don't fight her."

Mary Magdalene can tell that Peter isn't listening because something outside has caught his eye. She can't see what he is looking at outside the window.

"Enough!" she hears him shout as he barrels out.

"What's the matter?" John calls after him. Perplexed, Mary Magdalene goes to the window, and John joins her.

Mary Magdalene watches Peter storm outside, running down the exterior steps at a breakneck speed. He grabs the whip out of the master's hand and raises it to hit him. She fears that Peter will take out his anger at her on this man, now cowering in fear just as his slave had. She knows better than anyone that slavery is an evil practice, but slave owners won't be converted by force.

She hears Peter shout at him, "Coward!"

"Please," the master fearfully begs him.

Mary Magdalene calls from the window, "Peter! No!" She sees Peter hesitate and begin to tremble. He finally throws the whip aside.

"Nothing—gives—you—the—right!" he exclaims pointedly.

Mary Magdalene hears the man whimper and watches Peter walk away. She lets out a sigh of relief and prepares for the argument that will occur once he returns to the room. Peter enters the upper room, and she can see that he is out of breath and anguished. He looks at her.

"Go ahead, say it."

"And what shall I tell you?"

"Let's have your opinion, whatever it is. You already walk around here like you're the leader of this community."

"Peter, the leader of this community is here. It's not me. And it's not you."

Peter looks at her defeated. He sits down and wipes his face.

"He appeared to you first. Why?"

"It's not for me to say. Isn't it enough that he's back?"

She sees Peter nod in concession. *Maybe now we can talk this out,* she thinks. Mary Magdalene gently pulls him aside.

"Jesus taught me that by turning my soul to God I could change and let go of the old ways."

"But what if feelings well up in you that you can't control?"

"Every day is a struggle for each of us. Why should you be different?"

"He wants me to teach, and I can barely read. He wants me to show the way, and I can barely walk."

Mary Magdalene looks at him sympathetically. "You don't have to blaze a trail. Just walk in his footsteps."

"I'm not like you, Mary. I don't have the words, and I speak haltingly."

Mary Magdalene places her hand on his shoulder. "Jesus didn't pick us because we're perfect, Peter. He chose us because we're not."

She watches Peter close his eyes and lay his head on her hand. She can tell he is struggling hard to hold back the tears.

She tells him firmly and lovingly, "You heard Jesus say he's sending us the Holy Spirit. And Isaiah wrote that the Spirit gives us wisdom, understanding, knowledge..."

Peter looks at her sadly. "And courage?"

Mary Magdalene laughs and says emphatically, "Yes."

"Even to me, Mary?"

"Especially to you Peter. But we must prepare for the coming of the Holy Spirit."

"How?"

LATER THAT EVENING the disciples sit on pillows in a circle around Peter and Mary Magdalene. Now that Peter has reconciled with her, she notices that the other men accept her in this unaccustomed position. Mary Magdalene has a plan, and she shares it with them.

"We should gather Jesus' teachings."

John answers, "We can do that here among those we have with us."

Mary Magdalene agrees but adds, "Many of his followers in Jerusalem have also heard him speak. They might have sayings to add. What's important is that we spread his teachings."

She turns to Peter, who says, "We'll go to the temple in the morning. Spread the word that tomorrow night there'll be a meeting here, and every Jesus follower in Jerusalem is welcome. Meanwhile, let's get everyone who is here at Susanna's together to pray tonight."

*I*N A ROOM in the temple, Saul gazes at Silas, taking measure. *How much can he be trusted? He's perhaps too eager to please the high priests.* He asks Silas his questions as Annas and Caiaphas look on.

"The old woman is Salome," Silas answers. "The young one is Mary Magdalene. The tall wealthy lady, I don't know. Most of these people are Galileans."

Saul congratulates him. "Good job, Silas. That will be all."

*T*HE VIEW OF dawn breaking over the temple always has a profound effect on Mary Magdalene. *Maybe I'm being provincial,* she smiles to herself. *Perhaps the natives of Jerusalem can take it for granted.* But for her, it's awe-inspiring to see the majestic sight of the temple's rich ochre-colored stones materializing out of the misty pink light like an ancient ship breaking through the fog. But today, of course, is different. Today a definite trepidation invades her usual sense of reverence.

Today they are courting danger.

As she and Mary of Bethany walk in stride together, Mary Magdalene casts an occasional glance behind. *Good,* she thinks, *Mary, Salome, and Susanna are shielding Miriam from the crowd. No doubt they, too, feel the same apprehension.* Mary Magdalene takes a deep breath and wills herself to remember that Jesus is walking to the temple with them this morning. *And if Jesus is with me,* she thinks, *whom then shall I fear?* They merge with a crowd of worshipers and are constantly being jostled as they make their way. The people around them are subdued.

The silence of the morning is broken by thunderous noise as six men open the huge golden gate to the temple.

Mary of Bethany exclaims, "The Nicanor Gate is being opened!"

Mary Magdalene nods, dejected. *The sound reminds me that we women are only allowed to go into the first court of the temple.* This is a usual sore point with her. It never fails to break the spiritual mood that the temple itself evokes in her.

The women move with the crowd across the Court of the Gentiles. They pass through easily and climb the steps to the Court of the Women. The men stop to throw coins into the trumpets, one of the many receptacles for temple offerings, and ascend another set of stairs to the Court of the Men.

As the worshipers await the high priest, they whisper verses from the Psalms and add their own prayers. Mary Magdalene and the women pause to reflect and worship. Mary Magdalene drinks in the moment as she hears the chorus of female voices around her.

Mary of Nazareth murmurs, "I praise your name for your mercy and faithfulness."

Susanna responds, "Lord, your mercy endures forever."

Mary Magdalene replies fervently, "Lord, will you abandon us, the creatures of your own hand?"

Suddenly a familiar face distracts Mary Magdalene from her prayers. Off to the side is Veronica, a tall, simply dressed woman in her twenties. Mary Magdalene remembers her from that horrible day on Calvary when Jesus carried his cross and the blood and sweat were pouring down his face. Veronica had been in the crowd, watching. She had moved forward quickly and wiped Jesus' face with her headscarf.

Mary Magdalene leans over to Veronica whispering, "There's a meeting tonight at Susanna's to share Jesus stories." Mary Magdalene looks around to see if she's being observed. "Will you come?" Veronica discreetly nods.

The crowd hushes when Annas, the high priest, enters high above them and begins to sing the Shema, a morning prayer in Hebrew.

"Hear Israel, the Lord is our God, the Lord is one. Blessed be the Name of his glorious kingdom forever and ever."

Mary Magdalene is swept up in the beauty of the prayer.

As THEY LEAVE the temple, Mary Magdalene can't help thinking how different this service has been from their meeting at Susanna's last night. As though reading her thoughts, Mary of Bethany grumbles that she could barely see and hear Annas.

"Yes," Mary Magdalene agrees. "At our meeting last night, men and women, slave and free, rich and poor—we all prayed together. We were one body just as we were when we walked with Jesus."

As the women walk through the Court of the Gentiles, the crowds jostle them. The moneychangers, now set up for the day's business, shout out to the crowd, trying to outdo each other.

"Best rates of exchange in town."

"Come to me! I'll do well by you!"

Mary Magdalene knows that these men play an important role in temple affairs because no currency is accepted here save that issued by the high priest.

Mary of Bethany leans in closer to Mary Magdalene, trying to continue their discussion, "I had the same thought. As a matter of fa—"

Something suddenly catches Mary Magdalene's eye. She sees Mara, a regal older woman, walking hurriedly and accompanied by two of her sons John Mark and Samuel. Walking behind the family is their slave, Rhoda, a large black woman.

"I'm sorry. Hold on, Mary. I'll be right back."

Mary Magdalene pushes through the crowd until she catches up to the taller woman. She gently grabs a hold of Mara's shoulders.

"There's a meeting tonight at Susanna's," Mary Magdalene whispers. "Would you spread the word at your end of town?"

Mara looks around warily to see who might have been listening and nods. As quickly as they came together, the two women separate. Mary Magdalene turns to see Mary of Bethany headed her way, leading a young woman by the hand.

"This is Esther, an old friend of mine from Bethany," Mary of Bethany says quietly, trying to make sure no one can overhear. "She's excited about the meeting."

Mary Magdalene says graciously, "You'll be very welcome, Esther."

*A*s MARY MAGDALENE and her friends cut through the mob, a temple guard views the crowd from a platform high above. A red-headed man is at his side.

It's Silas, acting as Saul of Tarsus' bird dog.

Silas is scanning the mobs of people. He knows she is here somewhere because he saw her leave. There are so many bodies in the courts below. Suddenly, Silas nudges the guardsman and points.

"There," as he gazes down at Mary Magdalene in the court. "She's the one you want."

*A*s MARY MAGDALENE and her friends reach the road outside

the entrance to the temple, they are startled by the loud blare of trumpets and the sound of galloping horses. In the distance they see Roman soldiers on their powerful horses and then a chariot with an imperial standard crossing the upper city followed by their retinue.

"That must be Pilate," a bystander says excitedly.

As the party gets closer, the trumpets continue to blare. The thunder of galloping horses mingles with the creak of chariot wheels.

Mary Magdalene watches with dread as the entourage takes a road toward the temple, passes below and then turns south towards the lower city. She can tell the women with her, who watched Jesus die, are upset by this parade of Roman arrogance. Miriam begins to cry, and Mary Magdalene puts her arms around her.

"Don't cry, Miriam. Rome is going to die. There's going to be a new Rome, and it will be ours." Mary Magdalene sees Miriam smile at the apparent absurdity of her statement. "Wait and see."

The feeling of dread dissipated, the women start to walk towards the steps when two temple guards appear in front of Mary Magdalene.

"You! Come with us." Then they point to Salome. "We want the old crone, too." Mary Magdalene looks with pity at Salome, who has begun shaking hard.

Panic flashes inside Mary Magdalene as she wonders, *Could the authorities have heard already about the meeting we're planning?* After turning to see the concerned faces of her fellow disciples, she grabs Salome's hand and follows the guardsmen back into the courts. *Dear God, she prays, Please don't let them find out who Joanna is. It will not go well with her and Chuza if they know.* She tries to get closer to Salome to whisper to her not to tell. At that moment, the soldiers move the women in opposite directions. Her heart goes cold. *Will Salome have the sense to keep what she knows to herself?*

$\mathcal{T}$HE OLD WOMAN falls as two guards throw her roughly into a bare room in the temple. Saul, who has been leaning against a table, picks her up with a show of concern.

"Mother, have they hurt you?"

Tears streaming down her face, the woman nods and shows him her hand. He examines it.

"And my bones hurt. I'm an old woman!"

"I'm going to have a talk with those brutes." He leads her to a chair and kneels beside her. "You've been through a lot, haven't you? I'm afraid I don't know your name."

She breaks into great sobs and whispers, "Salome."

"Salome, you watched Jesus being crucified?" She nods as the tears run down her cheeks. "And then you were at the tomb when he was anointed."

"No, he wasn't anointed. He wasn't there!"

Saul stands abruptly. "Where was he?"

"He came back to us as he said he would."

Saul is shocked and turns his face away from her. "You saw him?"

She answers, "Many saw him."

"Who went to the tomb with you?"

Salome blithely answers, "Mary Magdalene and Joanna, wife of Chuza."

"Chuza, Herod's steward?" She nods yes. Saul digests this information.

"I have to leave now, but I'll make sure the guards don't touch you again."

Saul watches her smile at his words. He leaves, closing the door behind him.

Turning to the guards he mutters, "I think I've got all I need out of this one."

*I*N ANOTHER COMPLETELY bare room in the temple, Mary Magdalene is pacing up and down. *We've just gotten things started. More and more people are learning about Jesus. Dear God, don't let this be the end for us. Jesus said we were to go throughout the world with his message. We're the mustard seed. If we are stamped out, who will spread his Word?* Her thoughts are interrupted by the sudden opening of the door.

A dominating man strides into the room, slams the door, and walks quickly to her.

"Who took the body?" he demands roughly.

Mary Magdalene answers defiantly, "No one. He rose."

He slaps her hard on the face. "You're lying!"

She recoils at first and then stares at him defiantly. "It was written in the psalm, 'Thou wilt not suffer thine Holy One to see corruption'—Jesus is the Messiah. He walks among us."

"Many men claiming to be the Messiah come through Jerusalem." His voice rises. His handsome features twist. "They are boils on the flesh of Judaism and must be lanced!"

She is horrified at his sudden rage. "Jesus came to fulfill the law. Are you the arbitrator of the law?"

The man moves so close to her that their faces are almost touching. She tries not to flinch. "Do not defy me, woman," His voice has dropped to a whisper—so low that it's even more menacing. "Because if you do, neither your beauty, nor the law, nor that Jesus you're so fond of, will stop me—Saul of Tarsus—from grinding you back into the Galilean dirt."

She watches him open the door and snap his fingers at the guards. "Release them." Then he turns to her. "I'm watching you."

Mary Magdalene comes out into the hallway and sees Salome. She pulls the older woman to her as they wait for a guard to show them out. She turns to see Saul, the menace, whisper something to another guard.

Chapter Seven

*M*ARY MAGDALENE IS lying on Joanna's bed in the house of the women. She seldom comes in this room—none of them do—but today is different. She is giving the first teaching at the meeting tonight, and she needs to think about what she will say. The room is appointed luxuriously, not as sumptuously as Susanna's bedroom, but quite elegantly nonetheless.

How much of my story should I share? Should I tell about my parents' sudden death in an epidemic that swept through Magdala? About how at fifteen—the age Miriam is now—I was left with a business to run? Yes, I had an overseer, a good and capable man, but I was expected to approve all decisions and be a part of the day-to-day running of the dye shop. It was too much for me. I see that clearly now. I lacked patience and kindness. I used to fly off the handle at any little thing.

One day had been especially bad.

Could I tell that story? How much should I share? I was awakened in the middle of the night when a male slave put his great hand over my mouth so my scream wouldn't be heard. When I awakened a second time, I wasn't really awake. I could see and hear but not speak. My body floated around the ceiling of the room. How long was I like that? It was weeks, at least. They fed me soup and gruel, she remembers.

And when I recovered, the slave was gone. Months later, I discovered he had been beaten and executed. How much of that was that my fault? It's a man's life. Had I provoked him with my behavior? She focuses herself back to the present because she needs to think about how she will frame this story to make listeners understand her culpability—and what Jesus gave her.

*T*HAT EVENING THE sound of music and singing drifts from Susanna's upper room to the street below. Saul paces up and down in front of the house, listening. His mind keeps going back to the prophecy that the woman had repeated—that God would not have allowed his Holy One to have become corrupted. He, who knows scripture backward and forward, is well aware of the prophecies concerning the Messiah. *She was clever to allude to this one. Yes, she is clever all right. Perhaps these Galileans should not be underestimated. At least not this one.*

*I*NSIDE THE UPPER room, Mary Magdalene spots a shock of red hair and then a pair of eyes watching her intently. Silas stands in the shadows; she watches him observing the assembly of believers invited by Mary Magdalene and her friends. A shiver runs down her spine.

Besides the apostles and disciples who are all here, Mary Magdalene sees that there are many new people. Some are well-dressed; some are obviously poor. Among them are Veronica, Esther, John Mark, Mara, Samuel, Rhoda, and Stephen, a slender twenty-year-old. There are now also a cantor and some musicians.

As she scans the crowd, she is startled when Gamaliel enters, returning for the second time. She and Peter had wondered if he would come because they had gotten word that yesterday he had put out the eye of his slave Tabi after accusing him of looking lustfully at his daughter. Both she and Peter abhor the practice of slavery, especially the cruel rights that masters have to punish their slaves for the slightest infraction. She hopes Jesus' words will soften Gamaliel's heart.

Her eyes drift back to Silas, who still stands on the sidelines, watching.

Mary Magdalene's focus shifts to Peter as he walks up to the front of the room. She can tell he has more confidence now but still speaks haltingly.

"Thank you all for coming," he says jovially. "We're especially happy to see so many new faces. Tell your friends that we are spreading Jesus' messages. Tonight is a special night because we're beginning what we call 'teachings,' opportunities for those who have walked with Jesus to explain how they came to believe in him. Mary Magdalene is the first. She'll tell you how she was brought to Jesus."

Mary Magdalene sees Peter gesture toward her, and she moves to the front of the room and looks out over the congregation. She sees Silas watching her intently. Her nerves flutter as she takes a breath.

"In Magdala, I worked as a dyer for my parents. They died suddenly in an epidemic, and I was left to run the shop..."

Old buried images—more vivid than ever—assail her mind as she tells her story:

A fifteen-year-old girl supervises the operation, wearing the heavy makeup and bright clothing that was fashionable at that time in Magdala.

On a platform, a tall, muscular man, clad in a loincloth, stirs a huge vat.

Another slave—a young serving girl in simple, rough garb—carries a heavy jar of dye to the vat. She drops it, smashing the jar and spilling the dye on the dirt floor.

She tries to push the images of that day out of her mind. They crowd in.

"It was a great deal of responsibility—more than I could handle. I was angry, anxious, and fearful all the time. I couldn't control my reactions."

Herself again at fifteen. She runs toward the girl and slaps her.

The sound of the slap still rings loudly in her ears. The memory makes Mary Magdalene pause and bow her head.

The male slave looks at her with hatred, a hatred he will act out later that night.

"I had no patience with others. I criticized and screamed at people."

Again, a vivid memory floods her mind.

Herself again, eighteen this time, in a field in Capernaum, dressed in the bright clothes and makeup that she wore in Magdala.

Jesus has his hands on her shoulders.

She breaks down into deep sobs and writhes on the ground, crying out her pain.

Jesus and his mother stand patiently on either side of her.

"I met Jesus and his mother, Mary, in Capernaum, a town near Magdala. He changed me and led me to peace. What he did for me, he can do for you."

She smiles beatifically. The crowd applauds. Mary Magdalene looks back into the dark corner where Silas smiles cynically. His face fades as her friends gather about her murmuring their congratulations and embracing her warmly. Caught up in the moment, Mary Magdalene feels exultant; she has done as Jesus asked by teaching others!

As she sees Peter take charge of the meeting, she remembers Silas's face and takes Susanna aside.

"Ask Silas if he's willing to be baptized. If not, he shouldn't be at the meeting."

Susanna is troubled. "You suspect."

"Yes."

Mary Magdalene notices the contrition fill Susanna's face. *I know she is thinking, "I should have listened to her when she spoke to me earlier."* She gently pats Susanna's hand. She turns to see that Silas is glaring at them as they whisper. She watches him turn and head for the door, where he almost bumps into Nicodemus, a member of the Sanhedrin.

Mary Magdalene, surprised to see the priest, is grateful that Peter spots him and moves forward to greet him.

"We didn't expect another member of the Sanhedrin here tonight," she hears Peter say.

Nicodemus, a dignified man with a pleasant demeanor, replies, "Jesus and I often talked."

Peter introduces Nicodemus to some newer followers. Mary Magdalene notices Silas slip out, and she moves over to Peter.

"Mary, did you see that Nicodemus is here?" Peter says. "And that young Stephen is very enthusiastic. Pretty good turnout."

"We need more. Tomorrow, I should go to people's homes and urge them to join us."

"I'll go with you."

*S*TILL LURKING IN the shadows in front of Susanna's house, Saul watches as Silas runs toward him. The familiar wave of revulsion washes through him. *Is it Silas himself or simply the fact that he is a spy that I loathe?*

"That Magdalene was teaching. She spoke to Susanna about me. I think she suspects. Oh, and it looks like a member of the Sanhedrin was there."

Saul is taken aback. "Who?" He had seen a man who looked like Gamaliel come in, but had immediately dismissed the idea.

"I didn't catch his name."

*S*AUL IS UNCOMFORTABLE lounging on a long pillow near Annas and Caiaphas in the opulent banquet room in Annas' palace. He hates the indolence and indulgence these high priests allow themselves. He's much more comfortable on his horse, leading men, or even making tents in the brisk air of early morning. He looks over at Annas and Caiaphas who are laughing as servants pour more wine and bring them yet another delicacy. Saul feels nothing but contempt for them. *That the high priesthood should have come to this! They are lackeys of Rome and just as sybaritic as the Romans.* His musings are interrupted by Annas' question.

"Tell us, Saul, what more have you found out about these Jesus followers?"

"The men are just as hysterical as the women. They believe

that Jesus rose from the dead."

Caiaphas snorts. "Ignorant Galileans. What would you expect?"

"They're not all ignorant. That woman from Magdala was sharp. Probably well educated. They had a meeting last night. Silas tells me she did what they call a 'teaching.'"

Annas asks, "What do you plan to do next?"

"We need to get them out of Jerusalem."

"Then perhaps it is time to get Herod involved."

Caiaphas jumps in, "Telling him about his steward's wife might be a start."

"Let me do that," Annas insists. "I can give him an earful."

*M*ARY MAGDALENE PULLS her shawl over her nose as she walks with Peter through the street of the tanners. Because of the foul odor, the tanning itself is done outside of Jerusalem's walls, but the men who ply that trade and their wives live in this poor district within the city walls, and they carry the smell with them.

The children, playing in the dirt street, wear rags and have an undernourished look about them. These are the people Jesus came to help, and she and Peter hope to get some of them at their meetings.

They approach a small house, and Peter knocks at the door and then stands back as a woman opens it.

Mary Magdalene says, "We're Jesus' followers. We're holding a meeting tonight at seven. Would you and your husband be interested in coming?"

The woman is obviously upset. "My husband is very sick. The doctors say they can do nothing."

"Perhaps we can help. May we take a look at him?"

Puzzled, the woman lets them in. Mary Magdalene turns to Peter, who seems equally puzzled. She enters the house where a man, who looks near death, lies on a mat in an otherwise bare room with a dirt floor.

Looking compassionately at the man, Mary Magdalene asks, "What do they say is wrong?"

"He has a huge growth in his stomach."

Mary Magdalene kneels, feels the man's stomach, nods, and rises. "Peter, shall we pray over this man?"

Peter kneels by the mat, places his hands on the man's stomach, and prays, "Jesus, in your holy name, heal this man."

Mary Magdalene joins in. "Heal him, Lord. Please heal him."

Then she says to the woman, "Did you know our Lord? Would you like to join us in prayer?"

Mary Magdalene sees the woman, who is near tears, kneel by their side and plead, "Jesus, please heal my husband. He's a good man, who has worked hard all his life for his family."

The man doesn't respond. Mary Magdalene looks at Peter and she watches his shoulders droop.

Peter says dejectedly to the woman, "Perhaps we have brought your husband some comfort. If my Master were here, he could do so much more for him."

Mary Magdalene smiles as the woman places her hand on Peter. Looking from one to the other, she thanks them for praying. As they leave, Mary Magdalene embraces the woman.

As Peter and Mary Magdalene sadly walk away, Peter says, "If only we had the power of Jesus."

"Perhaps we shall."

Peter looks at her questioningly.

"After the Spirit descends."

As they continue on their way, a pack of street dogs is in their path, tearing a goat to pieces. They walk around them, staring in horror as the animal dies. Mary Magdalene feels Peter shiver.

"Are you all right?" she asks, concerned.

"It's just a bad memory from the day Jesus died. I saw vultures feeding on the bodies of the men crucified with him. Will that be our fate, Mary?"

Mary Magdalene shakes her head to empty the images from her head. She looks at Peter and seeing his body slump with fear, she thinks, *What do the days ahead have in store for us?*

IT'S EARLY EVENING, and Peter is sitting on the exterior stairway leading to Susanna's upper room and feeling depressed. He's whittling a whistle. Stephen, a new disciple who caught Peter's attention the day before, comes and sits on a stair below him.

"Who are you making the whistle for?" he asks.

Peter answers reluctantly, "My son." Peter notices that Stephen seems surprised. "Your son? I didn't know you were married."

"My wife is dead." Peter tries to focus and concentrate on his whittling.

"How many children do you have?"

"Four sons and a daughter."

"Who's taking care of them?"

"My mother-in-law."

"How do they live?"

"The eldest runs my fishing business."

"How old is the boy you're making the whistle for?"

Peter looks up from whittling with tears in his eyes. "Eight." He stands and ruffles Stephen's hair. "You ask a lot of questions. You know that."

He goes on his way, unconcerned by the puzzled look he notices on Stephen's face.

Chapter Eight

*J*OANNA HEARS A timid knock on her back door. Manaen, Herod's foster brother who lives in the palace, stands before her, looking at her with grave concern.

"Manaen, since when have you come to the back of the house?"

Manaen looks furtive. "Things have changed, Joanna. I've come to warn you and Chuza."

"About what?"

"Herod's been ranting about the Jesus followers. He sees them as threats to his power."

Joanna murmurs, "Does he know you are one of us?"

Manaen shakes his head. "It was easy to be with Jesus while we were in Tiberias. Herod cares little for me, so he scarcely missed me and was satisfied with any excuse I gave for being away. It's different here in Jerusalem. I haven't dared to go to Susanna's."

"You're that worried?"

"I don't understand why you and Chuza aren't."

"We've been cautious. I haven't gone to Susanna's either."

"But you were with him when he died. You walked to Golgotha with him. Some have said you took Peter into Annas' courtyard the night before."

Joanna is taken aback. Even Chuza didn't know that. Suddenly, she feels a sinking sensation in the pit of her stomach. Chuza wasn't exaggerating. She had put them in great danger.

"Manaen, we grew up in the palace with Herod Antipas. He's known us since we were children. He would never hurt us."

"He has his soft side, but only when it costs him nothing."

"When the danger is over, will you be a Jesus follower then?"

"You don't have to go to meetings to be a Jesus follower."

As ANNAS APPROACHES the steam room he grumbles to himself, *Beastly Roman custom—men stripping naked, exposing themselves, and then sweating like pigs. Why not? That's what they are—rotten pigs—but we have to deal with them. Well, as long as they give me what I want! Pilate has. Now let's see how I'll do with this one!* He smiles to himself. *I've survived for thirty years; yes, not only survived but thrived. Four sons and a son-in-law succeed me, and, God willing, I'll live to see a fifth son as high priest. And who will be the power behind the throne? I will. Nobody is better at this than I!*

As he enters the baths, he pays the attendant and takes a towel from him. Looking from left to right, he sidles into the narrow booth and clumsily removes his robes and hangs them. The towel is skimpy, and he struggles to tie it. Looking down, he sees his withered body with its ribs exposed and then laughs to himself. *It's good that Caiaphas didn't take this job. This towel would never have fit around him!* Then he worries about finding Herod.

Finally, through the rising steam, he spots Herod, a towel carelessly wrapped around him and his genitals exposed. Cautiously, Annas moves toward him, uncertain of his reception. Annas notices that Herod is surprised to see him. Interesting.

"Annas? You've adopted the Roman customs?"

Fighting his embarrassment, he mutters, "You think more highly of the Romans than I do, my King. I would only come here for a matter of the utmost urgency."

Herod gives him a hard look. "Speak your mind."

"Treachery. Treason. As close to you as I now stand."

*C*HUZA PACES IN the hallway outside of Herod's throne room, waiting to be summoned. *Why would he want me to appear before him? What have I done? Is it about my work or could Manaen be right that he has discovered our allegiance to Jesus? Dear Jesus, help us. Why was I so stupid as to let Joanna be with them all that time? Why didn't I protect her better? It worked when we* *were in Tiberias and Sepphoris. She would spend the day with them and then would be back before anyone noticed. Who could have known that Jesus would be crucified? He was a healer, not a dissident.*

Suddenly, the large double doors to the throne room are flung open, and two soldiers Chuza hasn't seen before seize him roughly and indicate he should walk toward the ornately carved throne. Herod's face wears a menacing scowl as he glares at Chuza, who walks the gauntlet of two rows of soldiers at rigid attention. He bows.

"You sent for me, Excellency?"

"I see you've been very busy, Chuza."

"Yes, Excellency. I'm laying in supplies for the rest of our stay and getting things ready for the return to Tiberias."

Herod nods. "Important work for a steward. What else have you been doing?"

"Excellency?"

"Have you been vigilant about who's in the palace? It's come to my attention that I may have a traitor here."

Chuza is now worried. "A traitor, my Lord?"

"Yes. I need your help to root him out."

Chuza is wary now. "What has he done?"

"Supported the Galilean behind my back. Has this come to your attention? Have you noticed any signs of a Jesus follower around the palace?"

Chuza becomes more frightened. "No, my Lord."

"This snake does not act alone. I hear his wife supports a woman named Susanna who's running a house of sedition. Have you heard of such a woman?" Terrified now, Chuza shakes his head. "Come now, Chuza. Any information you have would be helpful. The identity of the woman, for instance."

Chuza kneels. "My Lord, I know of no woman who would betray your kingdom or your person."

"If you did, would you kill her for me?" Chuza is aghast. "You would, wouldn't you? I would expect you to. Speak up, Chuza."

Chuza rises and looks around at the soldiers. *There's no place to run.* "I'm a steward, my Lord, not a soldier or a murderer."

Herod cries out, "Guard, open the door!"

The door opens and Chuza gasps in horror. He sees Joanna gagged with her arms bound behind her back. Two soldiers have their lances at her back. She runs forward into Chuza's arms. As he unties the gag, she looks up at him with tears streaming down her face.

"I'm so sorry!"

Herod grabs a soldier's sword, pushes Joanna aside, and angrily applies it to Chuza's throat.

"My money. You used my money to support the very man who wanted my throne."

"My Lord, you misunderstand, he wanted no such thing. His kingdom is—"

"His kingdom. His kingdom! I should kill you this minute!"

Chuza pleads with him, "Have pity on us!"

"Was I the only one ignorant of your treachery? I'm going to give you lots of time to think about how much a fool you made me."

Chuza falls on his knees, and Joanna follows. "Antipas, in the name of our friendship and growing up together in your father's palace, I beg you to have mercy on us."

Herod's face darkens. "That was why I thought I had your loyalty but still you betrayed me!"

Chuza cries out, "Excellency no! You misunderstand!" His face twists in pain. "Do what you want with me, Excellency, but spare my wife. Please have mercy on her." Chuza kisses the hem of his garment.

"I did have mercy, Chuza, I could have had you and your traitorous wife crucified, but then everyone would have known I had a disloyal staff. I'm going to keep your disappearance very quiet."

Herod motions to the soldiers, who seize them roughly. As they take them away, Herod calls out, "Think about that while you rot in a cell. And think about what's to come."

$\mathcal{J}$OANNA'S BOY CROUCHES in an ornate tall chest hung with his mistress' robes and cloaks. Her familiar smell comforts him as he buries his nose in one of the robes. He had overheard only that they had been seized. *What does this mean? Will they be back?* He tears a hunk from the loaf of bread he had secreted with him, not knowing how long his wait might be and eats it hungrily. After a time he falls asleep, only to be awakened by the sound of unfamiliar voices.

He hears two men, laughing and joking, as they drop a heavy object in front of the chest. Then he hears a woman's voice, and the door opens. He quickly throws Joanna's robe around him, only to have it pulled roughly off. He is grabbed and thrown out to the floor, hitting his head on a trunk.

"Look what I've found here," the woman cries. "Who are you? Not their child from the looks of you!"

"Where are my master and mistress?"

"Not where you'll find them!" She laughs and a hatchet-faced man laughs with her. "Throw him out!"

The new steward grabs him by his collar and throws him out the door. "Get out of here and don't come around again."

Once again Joanna's boy is a street waif; his life of luxury, safety, and comfort has been short lived.

INSIDE HEROD'S PALACE in a prison cell, Joanna is wrapped in Chuza's comforting arms. *How could it have come to this?* she thinks. The stench of the place assails her; the cold seeps into her bones. There is not a shred of comfort, only a soiled mat and some pieces of straw. *Even animals live better than this.* The guard marches in front of the cell with his long sword in a scabbard by his side and looks in at them, leering. She buries her face in Chuza's neck and feels a stab of pain. *Chuza's goodness led us here—and my carelessness. Everyone knew the danger. Manaen certainly did. Why was I so blind? How could I have put this good man in this position?*

Looking up at him she says, "I never thought he would hurt me."

Chuza replies, "You forgot; he's his father's son."

*M*ARY MAGDALENE LOOKS with pity at Joanna's boy who is sitting on a pillow and eating hungrily. He's filthy from sleeping outdoors all night, but his news frightens her. *Where could Joanna and Chuza be? One thing's for sure, Joanna would never leave this boy to fend for himself once more.* She glances at Mary whose face is suffused with compassion as she listens to the boy's story.

"Their things are all still there. The master's cart and animals, his stallion, the mistress' trunks, her robes and cloaks haven't gone."

Puzzled, Mary of Nazareth turns to Mary Magdalene, "Do you think Herod has fired Chuza?"

"If that were the case, why wouldn't they have cleared out their things? Why wouldn't they have come here?" Mary nods in agreement.

The boy, looking from one to the other begs, "Please find them for me."

Mary and Mary Magdalene look at each other with concern.

*A*s she leads Mary to Herod's compound, Mary Magdalene masks her fear but can't censor her thoughts. *He's a dangerous man. He had John the Baptist beheaded on a whim as a reward for his wife's brazen daughter. If we anger him, he won't hesitate to punish us. I am pretty sure that we already have Saul of Tarsus and the temple guards watching us. Do we need another enemy?* She looks over at Mary, whose beautiful face is serene as ever. *She's put herself in my care. Dear Jesus, let me be doing the right thing. Protect us.*

As they reach the compound, a pack of wild street dogs, fighting over a carelessly thrown piece of meat, are in their path. The women sidle close to the outside walls so as not to bring themselves to the dogs' attention and slip through the entrance. Taking a chance that the large house near the palace is the steward's, they knock on the door, which is opened by a thin-faced, impatient woman.

Mary Magdalene says firmly, "We're friends of Joanna and Chuza. May we see them?"

The woman smirks. "They left yesterday."

She attempts to close the door, but Mary Magdalene stops her. "Did they say where they were going?

"I didn't talk to them."

"May I talk to the new steward?"

"He's in the palace." With that, the woman slams the door.

They stand dejectedly for a moment.

Mary Magdalene asks, "Do we dare try the palace?"

Mary says bravely, "With the Lord beside me, whom shall I fear?"

Mary Magdalene is comforted by Mary's assurance but wonders if this is really wise. Her experience with Salome in the temple jail reminds her that women can be treated as harshly as men. *Should I put Jesus' mother in a similarly dangerous position? But what other choice do I really have? I owe Joanna and Chuza so much. I can't simply accept their disappearance.*

The women go to the side entrance of the palace, and Mary Magdalene knocks at the door of the servant's entrance. A cold, hostile servant opens the door.

"I'd like to see Herod's new steward. I'm Mary Magdalene."

"And what is your business with him?

'I'll tell him that."

"Wait here. The steward is a busy man. I'm not sure he'll have time for you."

*I*T IS LATE afternoon. A number of apostles and disciples are walking in groups up the steep incline of the road to the Mount of Olives. Miriam, quite large now, is riding on a donkey that Cleopas is leading. The garment he is wearing is tied around the middle with rope.

$\mathcal{T}$HE NEW STEWARD stands before Herod's desk. "My wife tells me a woman was inquiring about Chuza. Now she wants to see me."

Herod stiffens. "Who is she?"

"Her name is Mary Magdalene."

"See her. Find out what she knows."

$\mathcal{T}$HE NEW STEWARD stands in the doorway with Mary Magdalene before him and Mary behind her. The man is thin, almost frail looking. Mary Magdalene thinks, *Why would Herod replace tall, capable Chuza with this man?*

She speaks up boldly, "Sir, we're looking for our friends, Chuza and Joanna."

"They left here."

"Without their things?"

The man asks abruptly, "Are you a Jesus follower?"

"Yes."

His eyes narrow.

"Was Chuza fired?"

"I was hired. That's all I know." Then he adds craftily, "Where do the Jesus followers live?"

Mary Magdalene evades the question by answering him firmly, "We've asked all our friends. No one has seen them."

"I can't help you either." He moves to shut the door.

Mary Magdalene cries out, "They wouldn't have left like this!"

He slams the door shut. Mary and Mary Magdalene stand dejected in front of the closed door.

Finally Mary speaks, "I think he knows where they are."

Not to be discouraged, Mary Magdalene suggests, "Let's talk to people around the palace and see what they know."

Mary looks up at the sky. "It's getting late. Where did Peter say to meet?"

"On the Mount of Olives." Mary Magdalene's face clouds over with worry. "Joanna and Chuza should be with us. Oh Joanna, Chuza, where are you?"

Mary whispers, "I'm afraid something terrible has happened to them."

$\mathcal{J}$OANNA HAS TAKEN the straw from the floor of the cell and is weaving a cross with it as Chuza looks on. As she weaves, she thinks about Jesus and all he suffered. *We're like him. We've been imprisoned. Will we be whipped also? Crucified?* Tears seep out of her eyes. *Am I crying for Jesus or for us?* She looks up at Chuza and feels a love for him that takes her breath away. *He knew. He knew how dangerous it was, yet he still let me follow Jesus.*

She holds up the finished cross, "We can use it when we pray."

Chuza smiles and embraces her.

Chapter Nine

*A*s MARY MAGDALENE and Mary hurry up the steep ascent of the Mount of Olives toward Bethany, they pass a plateau on which stand two tall cedars. Under one of them are four small shops, belonging to sellers of things necessary for the purification sacrifices—lambs, sheep, doves, oils, and meal—sold at a price considerably lower than in Jerusalem.

Mary Magdalene reflects on the times Jesus chose the Mount of Olives for meetings, *Perhaps because it is so close to Bethany where he so often visited with his friend Lazarus and his sisters, Mary and Martha. He came through here on a donkey as he rode to Jerusalem. And this is where he asked the men to meet him on the night he was arrested.* The familiar stab of pain assails her as she thinks of that night.

Passing some rocks at the side of the road, she turns to Mary, "Let's stop here for a moment to rest."

They sit and gaze down on Jerusalem, which looks like an impregnable fortress from this vantage point. The temple rises up in all its splendor with its towers reaching toward the blue sky. Behind the immense Antonia Tower lays the old town; the houses huddle together in an ochre mosaic. Toward the west rise the palaces of the Hasmoneans with their white roofs and marble colonnades shining in the sun. Beyond that is the dark line of the city wall climbing toward the top of Mount Gareb. The scene takes the women's breath away and restores them for the steep climb ahead. As they climb, Mary Magdalene looks up at the late day sun.

"Look," she says to Mary, "the sun has a rainbow around it." The sight of this phenomenon fills her with wonder and hope.

Finally, passing through groves of luxuriant olive trees, they reach the flattened ridge of the mountain where the apostles and disciples are seated on the ground. Mary Magdalene sees Peter standing before them. The women find a grassy area, sit, and listen to Peter as he speaks.

"This is a sacred spot for us. Here Jesus spoke to us of the end times. And here he told us that heaven and earth will pass away, but his words will never pass away." He pauses on this and gives them time for reflection. "Let us sit now and pray on this sacred spot."

How assured he is now, Mary Magdalene thinks and feels a surge of pride in Peter whom she has grown to love very dearly. *This is why Jesus chose him. Once he bonds people to himself, they will follow him anywhere.* They pray quietly.

Suddenly—Jesus appears, quietly, instantly, and seemingly out of nowhere. The group erupts with simultaneous exclamations of joy.

Mary Magdalene cries out, "Lord!"

Mary exclaims, "My Son!"

Peter says in a low voice, "Jesus."

Some simply bow to the earth in reverence. Many of the others shout their praise. Jesus smiles at their delight. Mary Magdalene looks at Jesus and wonders what he will show them now. She sees James step forward and knows he has something he wants to say.

James asks eagerly, "Lord, has the time come?"

Matthew chimes in, "Are you going to restore your kingdom Israel?"

"When and where that happens will be decided by the Father, but you must always remember that the kingdom of God is within you and among you."

Mary Magdalene notices James and Matthew look crestfallen.

Seeing their disappointment, Jesus assures them, "Soon the Holy Spirit will come upon you and you will be given many powers. Then you will be my witnesses, not only in Jerusalem, but throughout Judea and Samaria and to the ends of the earth." He looks around as if he is saying goodbye to each of them, "You have touched my heart with so much love. Now the time has come for me to leave you and go to my Father."

Mary Magdalene's heart sinks with these words. Suddenly Jesus is suffused with a bright light that radiates up toward the heavens and out covering the promontory. Shading her eyes, she watches as the light engulfs him, lifts him up, and takes him from her sight.

Mary Magdalene notices Miriam crossing from her left. She has a wonderstruck look on her face as she runs toward the spot where he appeared and lifts her arms to the heavens. When she turns back to the crowd, she looks bereft. Mary Magdalene watches Cleopas, who has followed her gently, lead Miriam back to where they had been seated.

Mary Magdalene looks around at her companions. Unwilling to break the spell of wonder that has been cast, the believers who speak to one another do so quietly, recognizing that this ascension has been a sacred moment. Others simply sit still to absorb the enormity of what they have seen. Suddenly Mary Magdalene sees someone stand. It's Peter.

"Lord!" he cries. "Why do you leave us?"

Mary Magdalene sees the doubt written on his face, and she knows he is feeling puzzled, overwhelmed and alone. She bows her head and prays for him. She feels a hand on her shoulder and turns to see Nicodemus, visibly awed by this sight.

"I remember a prophecy in Psalms," he says with his voice distant and light. "'Thou hast ascended on high that the Lord God might dwell among them.'"

Mary Magdalene smiles, absorbing the promise of the psalm. She squeezes Nicodemus' hand in gratitude. This is confirmation of his promise that he will be always with them. In wonderment, she turns to embrace Mary and sees that the mother's face is lit by joy.

Mary Magdalene remembers all she and Jesus have meant to each other: the touch of his hand as they walked, the delicious moments of joy at shared jokes, and their conversations about Hellenistic thought that sprang from their experiences—hers gained in Magdala and his in Sepphoris where he worked. They were soul mates. She recognized his every mood. He was always aware when she was depressed and unhappy.

She glances at Thomas and sees that he looks troubled. He returns her glance, and she can tell he is trying to decide what he should do and if his job here is done. She tries to give him an encouraging look. As if to reassure him and herself, she thinks, *Now Jesus, the man, is gone to his Father in heaven. He has been taken from our sight so that he might be with us wherever we are.* But once more the troublesome thoughts intrude, *If he is the Son of God, why then isn't he God as well? And he is sending the Holy Spirit, his spirit. Are all three God?* The mystery of the man/God deepens for Mary Magdalene.

As if awakened from a trance, Mary Magdalene hears some of the disciples speaking of their feelings of loss. Their voices rise as they vent their disappointment. Sensing the confusion that is breaking out around her, she decides to stand.

"I've been asking myself why he came to us while praying and then left us again so quickly. It might be his way of telling us that we are ready to do as he asks."

She looks around at their faces to read the response and sees Peter rise. He nods at her, and she smiles back.

"Mary Magdalene is right. We shouldn't be disappointed. He's told us that he will be with us always in our struggles and our successes, and he's promised to send the Holy Spirit to us and to bestow on us many gifts. This is the beginning of the fulfillment of all his promises to us."

Suddenly two angels appear at the spot where Jesus has ascended.

"Jesus has been taken up from you into heaven," announces one of them. "He will come back in the same way. Be prepared for that day!"

The angels disappear as abruptly as they came.

As THE DISCIPLES walk down the steep hill from Mount Olivet, the sky goes from peach to purple and then to black lit by hundreds of stars and a brilliant full moon. As they walk, they become more and more buoyant and joyful. Jesus made them many promises: to send the Holy Spirit, to fill them with new powers, and one day to return. They have only to wait. There is so much good news to spread.

Mary Magdalene is once more lost in thought; *Jesus now belongs to the upper world of light and glory. He has promised that he will walk with us and be our advocate to the Father. So invisibility increases his power in the world to be with everyone everywhere. The angel said that at some future time he will descend from the heavens once more as a living man. What will happen then?*

*M*IRIAM, HOPING TO see the temple at sunset, is disappointed because it is a mere shadow in the darkness. *Remember the real light is within me and within the infant kicking at my sides with every step the donkey takes.* She takes a deep breath and then another, marveling to herself how fresh the air is. *Why I wonder is the air so different up here? In Jerusalem, there are so many unpleasant smells.* Then she pictures the streets crowded with people and animals of all kinds. She takes another deep breath and realizes that the deep breathing helps with the discomfort she feels as the kicks become more frequent and seem to reach deep within her.

*M*ARY MAGDALENE, HAVING been lost in the wondrous ascension of her Lord into heaven, remembers her concern about Joanna and Chuza. *Now,* she thinks, *is a good time to thread through the crowd, to ask people if they have any idea where they might be.*

*S*ITTING ON THEIR mat with their heads bowed inside the cell in Herod's palace, Joanna and Chuza are quietly praying. Joanna is holding up the straw cross so that it catches the one ray of light that seeps through the slit in the stone wall. It's the only way they can tell day from night in this dark hole.

Chapter Ten

*I*N THE HOURS before dawn at Susanna's house, the crickets and birds murmur, sing, and crackle in anticipation of the coming of a new day. Suddenly, their music is shattered by a loud scream.

Susanna is peacefully sleeping in her lavish bedroom with rich window hangings and an oriental rug on the floor. Her bed stands on legs, and the covering is heavily embroidered.

There is another loud scream. Susanna bolts upright, then smiles, and rises.

*I*N HER GROUND-FLOOR room, Miriam doubles over in pain and turns to her husband.

"Cleopas! It'll be soon."

"What do I do?"

"Get Mary!"

She lets out another loud scream.

*C*LEOPAS RUNS THE long distance to the house of the women. The empty streets increase his sense of anxiety. He feels impatient with himself. *I should feel joy, but I'm terrified. What if Miriam dies in childbirth as her mother did? I couldn't look at a child who cost me my precious wife. Why did I lie with her so soon? She was only twelve. At least we had three carefree years. It's still too soon for her to give birth. I'll lose her. Why didn't I wake Susanna so that at least she would have a woman with her? I left her all alone. God, what was I thinking?* A wild dog darts across his path, and he falls over it. His hands are bleeding as he redoubles his efforts to reach Mary.

*D*AY IS BREAKING, and Miriam's screams can still be heard periodically between the low moans and the encouraging murmurs of the women. Sitting on the ground under a tree outside the downstairs room are Cleopas, John, and Peter. Cleopas can't look at the other men and just shakes his head at Andrew, who comes bearing a loaf of bread and offers him a piece. Cleopas watches Andrew break the bread and give pieces to the other men who eat them hungrily. He can tell that they are all uncomfortable with his anxiety.

To break the silence, Andrew asks, "How long has she been in labor?"

Cleopas says pitifully, "Seven hours. The women have been with her for four." He then puts his head in his hands, sick with guilt, thinking. *For three hours she endured that agony with only Susanna by her side. I could have been with her. Why didn't I awaken one of the men and send him to fetch Mary and Mary Magdalene?* Cleopas stands and looks at the door to the room.

"I'm going in there. Miriam needs me."

He feels a tug at his arm and looks down at Peter, who grips his sleeve tightly. "No, Cleopas, you're not needed. Let the women do their work."

$\mathcal{T}$HE LANTERNS' DIM glow and the thin shards of light streaming through the narrow slits make the shadows cast by the women loom large against the walls of the dark room. Mary Magdalene and Susanna hold Miriam up as she clings to a rope fastened to a ceiling beam. Beneath her, Mary sits on a stone and massages Miriam's swollen belly, gently prompting the infant within to make his appearance. The contractions get harder and harder until at last there is one long shriek.

At the sight of the emerging head, the women begin ululating.

*I*N A PRISON cell inside Herod's palace, Chuza and Joanna, holding the cross, are kneeling facing each other, praying, "Our Father, who art in heaven, hallowed be thy name."

*H*EARING THE SOUND of ululating, the men stand expectantly. Cleopas makes another move to go in, but Peter restrains him. The pitch of the ululating rises.

Then all the women chant to God, "Yah! Yah! Yah! Yah! Yah!"

*A*S JOANNA AND Chuza continue praying in their cell, Joanna *really* listens to the words of the prayer.

"Thy kingdom come, Thy will be done on earth as it is in heaven."

What is your will for us Lord? To stay here for years? Or will you miraculously release us from this hell?

They stop praying abruptly when they hear heavy footsteps and the clank of swords.

Frightened, they look up as two of Herod's soldiers enter the cell and seize them. Joanna thinks, *Is this your time to release us Lord?* Chuza breaks away and attacks the man holding Joanna.

"Run Joanna!" She quickly runs out of the cell toward the stairs. She glances back to see the second soldier seize Chuza. As Joanna reaches the steps, the first soldier pierces her in the back with his sword.

She stumbles and cries out, "No!"

Grimacing in pain, she watches Chuza struggle but fall as the second soldier's long knife stabs him. The soldier reaches down and stabs him again. Joanna crawls to her husband and stretches her hand out to his. As she clasps it, the first soldier sinks his sword into her back once more.

$\mathcal{M}$ARY OF NAZARETH comes out into the bright sunlight with the peaceful infant in her arms. The baby squints his eyes and raises his little fists as if to seize the light. Cleopas eagerly holds out his arms and looks at her questioningly. Mary hands the baby to his father.

"It's a boy," she says tenderly.

Cleopas, eyes welling with tears, takes his son. "Thank you, Mary. We decided if he was a boy, we would call him David."

"Jesus' line. He'll like that."

Mary remembers the first time she held her son in her arms—and the last time. Her joy in this new life is dimmed by the realization that she will never hold a grandson of her own. *Please God, let this child have a peaceful life.*

Cleopas shows the baby to the three men who crowd eagerly around him, murmuring their congratulations. Then, he asks Mary, "May I see Miriam now?"

Mary nods.

As Cleopas goes in, Mary sees Mary Magdalene and Susanna

stoop through the low doorway of the little room, carrying bowls, jars, and bundles of soiled cloth. She watches Peter and Andrew follow them as they move toward the kitchen entrance.

Mary sits on the ground next to John and leans her back against the tree.

"You must be tired," John says with concern. She shakes her head.

"You and I have watched Jesus perform many miracles, but none is greater than the miracle of birth."

John nods in agreement.

"I wanted to talk to you about something, Mother. I had a terrible dream last night. One of our women was in an arena with lions."

Mary asks, "What do you suppose it means?"

"Perhaps nothing. I was awakened by Miriam's screams."

Mary tells him, "Well, Daniel went in the lion's den, and they all peacefully lay down," but privately she thinks, *The Romans just killed my son. What else are they capable of doing?*

John tries to understand the expression on Mary's face, but can only guess.

INSIDE HIS OFFICE in the palace and working at his desk, Herod looks up as a soldier with blood on his legs is admitted.

"It's done."

"Dispose of their bodies. I don't want them to be found—ever."

The soldier nods and leaves.

MARY AND JOHN are relaxing under the tree outside the ground floor room when Cleopas comes out, still carrying David.

"Miriam would like to see you, Mary."

AS CLEOPAS AND Mary leave, a messenger boy enters the courtyard and sees Uriah, who is stirring a pot on the stove of the outdoor kitchen.

"May I see Susanna, wife of Solomon?"

Uriah runs into the house and Susanna comes out. The boy hands her a letter written on rolled papyrus and tied with a cord and leaves hurriedly. Susanna breaks the seal, unrolls it, and frowns as she reads it.

MARY AND CLEOPAS enter the dark room. The lamps throw their shadows. Miriam sits in the center with a solemn look on her face. The robe, dirty and bloodstained, is on her lap.

Mary quietly sits opposite her. Miriam hands her the robe. Mary looks at it and begins crying. She fondles it, holds it up to her face, and buries her face in it. Her sobs rise in intensity. Miriam and Cleopas are crying also. Only David sleeps peacefully.

Chapter Eleven

*E*ARLY THE NEXT morning, Susanna hurries up the steep road to the Garden of Gethsemane. She is red faced, sweating, and breathless from the exertion. She remembers that this is where Jesus prayed on the night before he died and feels a terrible sense of foreboding. She takes one of the paths and penetrates deep into the foliage. Finally she stops at a bench, sits, and wipes her brow. Presently a voice from the trees and brush behind her calls her name.

Susanna rises and moves to the rear of the brush, facing a man in priestly garb who is hidden among the trees and bushes.

Susanna breaks the silence, "You sent for me?"

"You're in great danger."

"Why would I be in any danger? The ones I'm really concerned for are our friends; Chuza, Herod's steward, and his wife, Joanna. They are missing."

The priest in a level but clearly impatient voice answers, "I've heard nothing about them."

"Could you ask around the temple? Perhaps someone knows."

"Forget them! You need to worry about yourself. Your house is being watched. You're no longer safe."

"I've provided hospitality to my friends. I've done nothing wrong."

The priest moves out of the brush and grasps her arm. They are face to face. He speaks angrily to her now, "You've provided them with a meeting place. You've supported them out of your resources. Some say without you they would have dispersed weeks ago."

She shakes off his hand and backs away saying, "You give me too much credit."

He persists, "The sounds of singing and preaching in your upper room can be heard from the street. It must stop."

"We're meeting to pray. Surely they're not against prayer?"

His voice rises, "There are laws against people meeting after sundown. You must know that!" The priest is exasperated by her obtuseness. "I promised your husband I would protect you, but I can't any longer. Goodbye, Susanna."

As he leaves, the reality hits Susanna that she has no protection now.

SUSANNA AND MARY Magdalene are standing at the office window overlooking Susanna's back garden. Mary Magdalene looks with concern at Susanna, who is clearly agitated.

Susanna whispers, "His threat was serious."

"You've been very brave to host so many for so long."

"I'm worried about handling the feast of Pentecost!"

"You need to do what you think is right. But first, you have to get rid of Silas."

"Before Pentecost?"

"We'll manage without him. He's not to be trusted."

LATER THAT AFTERNOON, Silas is before Susanna, who is standing behind her desk with a bag of money in her hand.

He says to her insolently, "Haven't I served you well?"

"You've served others better. Here's your money. Clear out your things."

"You need me to run this madhouse. You'll see!"

"Uriah will make an excellent steward."

SILAS PACKS HIS bags while Uriah watches. Among the articles are some fine linens to which he has helped himself. He then tosses the bag of money Susanna just gave him to Uriah.

"It's up to you, now."

*I*N A ROOM in the temple, Saul angrily circles the table around which Annas, Caiaphas, and Silas are seated. He looks with contempt on the men in front of him.

"You're wasting my time!" Silas cringes, but the two priests hardly blink. "You brought me here weeks ago to get those extremists moving. When are you going to let me loose on them?"

Saul notices that Caiaphas is unfazed by his anger.

"The woman who houses them will be arrested after Pentecost when all the good Jews have gone home," Caiaphas replies.

Saul hears Annas say smugly, "That should get them on their way."

He has no time for their optimism. "They'll find other places to stay."

"There are too many of them for that," Annas insists. "They'll go back to Galilee."

"And I'm going back to Damascus if you keep tying my hands." Saul looks right at Caiaphas as he makes this threat.

"Pilate wants this to be done as quietly as possible—no civil unrest. Silas, what else have you found out?"

"That Magdalene suspected me. I need a new position."

Saul looks at him in disgust and makes a move to go.

He recognizes that Silas is trying to calm him by saying blithely, "There's no problem. I hired Uriah to take over." This makes Saul angrier still.

He looks hard at Annas and Caiaphas. "I'll give you a week.

Act or I leave!" As Saul walks out, he notices Annas and Caiaphas look at each other in alarm.

$\mathcal{P}$ETER AND MARY Magdalene are seated at the table in Susanna's office; Mary Magdalene looks with concern at Susanna who is pacing the room. Finally Susanna turns and gives them her decision.

"I'm going to go ahead with our plans for Pentecost."

Mary Magdalene shakes her head. "Are you sure? You could be in great danger."

"I'm sure." Susanna is emphatic. "My husband, God rest his soul, braved many dangers to make his fortune. The prize I seek is worth so much more than money."

Peter states matter-of-factly, "We all risk arrest."

Mary Magdalene agrees. "Yes, we all need to move."

Peter suggests, "We can start by breaking into smaller groups."

"Esther lives alone. She might be willing to take Mary, Salome, and me."

"The houses should be throughout the city. If one house becomes unsafe, there would be others to go to."

Mary Magdalene, fearful for Peter's safety, asks, "You're planning to stay?"

"My mission is to preach in Jerusalem."

Susanna is alarmed by this idea, "Peter, no! It's too dangerous."

"Jesus said, 'Unless a grain of wheat dies, there will be no harvest.'"

Mary Magdalene looks at Peter with admiration and awe. *He no longer can question his courage.*

CLEOPAS AND MIRIAM carry David who is wailing loudly as he has just been circumcised. They exit through the women's door of the temple. Miriam puts him over her shoulder and makes soothing sounds as they walk down the first flight of stairs, stopping at the broad landing below.

Miriam says lovingly to the baby, "Hush, David. This is your name day, love."

Cleopas asks, "Let me hold him, Miriam." Miriam hands Cleopas the baby who immediately stops crying. They both laugh delightedly.

"See, he knows who his father is."

As they move down a second long flight of steps, Cleopas talks to the baby, "You are now officially a member of the Jewish faith, a true son of your father Abraham."

They continue across the plaza area of the temple, which is crowded with the usual groups of worshippers, bird and animal sellers, and moneychangers. Cleopas notices one of the temple pools to his right. He nudges Miriam, and they walk over to it and pay the attendant. They then descend the broad steps.

Cleopas sits on the wide area next to the pool, looks down at his son, dips his hand into the water, and draws a cross with the water on his forehead.

"David, we dedicate you to the Father who gives us life, his son Jesus who died for love of us, and the Holy Spirit whom he promises to send."

Miriam beams with delight.

SUSANNA LOOKS DOWN at her desk where her treasures are laid out—gold necklaces; bracelets; rings; and the most prized of all, her Golden Jerusalem, a crown she would wear only on the most important occasions. It's pure gold and studded with precious gems from all over the world. All had been given to her by her husband, Solomon. He had been as wise as King Solomon but so much more—bold, daring, funny, and happy. He had been friend to any and all. These had been the qualities that had made him one of the wealthiest merchants in Jerusalem.

There also had been nothing he didn't dare do. He had gone to Arabia; rented two hundred camels and drivers; and brought back untold riches, spices, precious stones, gold, copper, iron, and most important, incense for the temple. From Babylonia he had imported lush materials in blue, scarlet, and purple and fine white linen. In Greece he had purchased beautifully decorated, hand-painted vases like the ones that had previously been in her office.

Yes, he had been successful, but that meant nothing to her beside his most precious quality: he had loved, adored, and cherished her. Never had a woman been made as happy by a man. When she had walked into a room, his face had lit up. And in their bedroom, magic had happened night after night when he had been home. How she had pined for him when he had been on his long journeys. She had felt her heart would break until he had come back to her arms again. Their one unhappiness had been that she was barren.

Any other man would have taken another wife or even wives but not Solomon. Nothing had meant as much to him as she had. Even when she had grown heavier and dreaded that he would reject her, he simply had said there was more of her to love.

She looks at the jewelry around her sadly. Parting with these gifts he had given her breaks her heart, but it has to be done.

Her reverie is broken by the knock on her door. Mary Magdalene enters, and Susanna watches her eyes focus first on the glitter of the jewels spread out on the desk. Susanna hears her exhale a long sigh, and she knows Mary Magdalene has never seen such a display of wealth.

"They're beautiful!"

"Yes, they were gifts from Solomon. I want you to take them to a jeweler friend of mine. He will be expecting you."

"But why, Susanna?"

"I won't be needing them," she states factually and then playfully adds, "I'm no longer invited to the fine homes where adornment is expected, nor do I want to be." She rises from the desk and puts her arms around Mary Magdalene. "Think of all our needs now, Mary. With everyone splitting up, we won't be providing for them. They will all need a purse for their travels."

Mary Magdalene looks quickly around the room thinking, *Yes, many more things are gone. How had I not missed the Greek vases before now?* Susanna sees Mary Magdalene's eyes well with so much love that the tears flow down her cheeks.

"Susanna, you've given so much."

"Not as much as my Lord. He gave so much more."

*M*ARY MAGDALENE GAZES around the upper room, feeling proud of how beautifully they have decorated it. There are tall vases of flowers everywhere, and garlands of flowers ring the tall windows. The early morning sun streams into the room, making the bowls on the tables piled high with fruit glitter.

If Jesus could only be here how pleased he would be. But he is, of course he is. She closes her eyes and imagines him walking about the room. He loved this ancient feast that commemorated Moses' giving of the law on Mount Sinai. It was celebrated fifty days after the Passover, the liberation of the slavery from Egypt. On Pentecost* God gave Moses the Ten Commandments and made

---

* Pentecost, which means "50th," is the Greek word for this holiday. The Hebrew word is Shavuot, which means "weeks." It was also called the "Feast of Weeks" since it was seven weeks after the Passover.

the covenant with his people.

She calculates that there are about one hundred and twenty persons assembled, standing, talking, and waiting for the meeting to begin. A cantor softly sings a hymn taken from a psalm.

"I will praise your name forever, my king and my God. The hand of the Lord feeds us and answers all our needs."

Looking more closely she notices that among the assembly are the priests Gamaliel and Nicodemus, and she wonders why Susanna's servant Uriah is simply watching the crowd. *Why isn't he downstairs with the other servants preparing the food for the feast?*

She makes her way to Peter and the apostles at the front of the room and stands beside Peter, who is facing the congregation. Looking up at him, she marvels at how much more confident he is now. *He is beaming at everyone, enjoying every minute, and looking refreshed even though I know that he and most of the other men have stayed up all night studying the Torah and reliving the revelation on Mount Sinai. Although he hasn't lost the halt in his voice, it is much less noticeable. He has truly assumed the mantle he has been given.*

Mary Magdalene hears Peter say, "Jesus is gone now from our sight, but his power and presence are with us." The people smile and nod with delight at this idea. "He told us that we're to go throughout the world and preach the good news to everyone everywhere."

Again the people murmur and talk among themselves. She watches the different reactions.

One man shouts out, "You want me to leave my home?"

"Not all of you. Just those who have the call."

A second man asks, "Will we be able to perform miracles as he did?"

Mary Magdalene now addresses the crowd. "Miracles are acts of faith. Brothers and sisters, do you believe that Jesus will be with us always?"

The crowd responds with a rousing "Yes!"

She sees Peter smile at their enthusiasm and hears him tell them, "Those you wish to heal must have faith also. So you must preach the Way to them and baptize. How many of you have this call?" Hands go up. "Will you come to the front of the room?"

Mary Magdalene smiles as five men go to the front and two of the apostles step forward. Peter is pleasantly surprised and clasps each one to him. Two women also go up, Mary of Bethany and Esther. Peter stops in amazement before the two women.

"You, Mary?" Like Peter, Mary is much more confident now even though her friend Esther looks hesitant.

"Yes, Peter. Esther wants to go, too."

"It's too dangerous for two women to travel alone."

Bartholomew, who is easily the tallest and largest man in the room, steps forward. "They could travel with Philip and me. They'd be safe with us."

Peter agrees and then turns to the crowd. "I have asked Mary Magdalene to speak to us about the Holy Spirit whom we await."

The people clap and cheer in response.

Mary Magdalene joyfully tells them, "Jesus said, 'I am in the Father, and the Father is in me. Before Abraham was I AM. I will send the Holy Spirit, who will dwell within you, teach you, and empower you.' Now let us praise and thank God in song!"

As she says this, she notices Uriah thread through the crowd, making his way toward the outside stairs. Her attention is diverted as the cantor and people sing a hymn from a psalm.

"Send forth your Spirit, O Lord and renew the face of the earth.

"Bless the Lord, O my soul, O Lord how great you are!"

Peter with great joviality invites the crowd. "Let's eat the feast Susanna has prepared for us, rejoice, and thank God for his blessings."

Mary Magdalene watches Susanna's servants enter with trays of food and wine. She sees one of them lean in and hears him ask Uriah, "Where have you been? The mistress was asking about you."

He replies curtly, "I had to do a head count, didn't I?"

Mary Magdalene is puzzled by this, but she is distracted by the people talking among each other as the food and drink is served and the musicians play their instruments. Just then a woman with a child in her arms hands her to Mary Magdalene.

Her husband explains, "Our daughter is very ill with a fever."

"Mary, please pray for her recovery."

Mary Magdalene looks down at the beautiful child and feels that her head is hot to the touch. *Dear God, help these poor parents.* Mary

Magdalene then prays aloud as she was asked, "Come Holy Spirit, with your grace and heavenly power, heal this precious child."

As she finishes this prayer, the sound of a rushing wind whips around the building and then seems to blow through the room. A pitcher on a table crashes to the floor, and the fruits heaped in bowls roll off. People's garments wave around them. The women's scarves blow off; their hair is raised. A tray of mugs, carried by a servant, is whipped out of his hand; beverages spill; and mugs clatter to the floor. The people look out and then around in amazement.

The room shakes. Mary Magdalene's amazement turns to fear. She clutches the child to her while the parents hold each other.

The wind turns into a huge ball of fire on the ceiling. She sees some react in alarm, fall to the floor, and cover their heads. *Jesus help us understand,* she prays.

She watches as one woman raises her arms against it, shouting, "No! No!"

A man shouts, "Fire! Fire!"

Others show reverence and awe. The fire separates and dances around the room. It seems to envelop and play among the people in little tongues. Several people reach out to feel it.

Others caution, "Don't!"

One woman touches it saying, "It looks like fire but feels like warm flesh."

Tongues of fire then sit upon each one of them who is a believer and is prepared to receive the Spirit. Mary Magdalene looks up and observes her companions with awe. She sees others, including Uriah, move to the periphery of the room and watch. Simultaneously the faithful begin speaking out loudly in foreign tongues.

Mary Magdalene cries out in Persian, "It's the Holy Spirit!"

She remembers Jesus' words and is filled with excitement. *This is what we've all been waiting for. What will this mean for us?* Looking down at the child in her arms, *How will we be changed? What will we be challenged to do?*

In a loud voice in Syrian, Peter affirms her. "The Holy Spirit is upon us."

Miriam cries out in Greek, "It is as Jesus promised. He has sent the Holy Spirit." She and Cleopas embrace with their baby gurgling between them.

Then, prompted by the Holy Spirit, those who are gifted begin speaking in other languages, which all present can understand even as they speak in their own.

Mary Magdalene hands the child back to her mother who feels her forehead and then says in Arabic, "Her fever is gone!"

The child's father responds also in Arabic, "We can never thank you enough."

Mary Magdalene smiles and continues in Arabic, "Thank you for your faith."

They suddenly realize they have just held a conversation in another language. They look at each other astounded and then can't help but burst out laughing. Mary Magdalene prays silently, *Thank you, Lord.*

Thank you for this astonishing gift. Make me worthy of it.

Mary Magdalene moves toward Peter and overhears him speak in Greek to Nicodemus, "Nicodemus, I'm so happy you were here to witness this."

Nicodemus motions to Gamaliel. "Gamaliel, listen to Peter! He's speaking Greek."

Mary Magdalene marvels at the different languages that her friends are speaking around her. She hears Mary of Nazareth speak in Egyptian to John, and he answers her in that language. Mary of Nazareth then exults in Persian, "I have lived to see this."

Replying to her in Persian, John says, "Jesus, our God and Savior."

Mary Magdalene observes Gamaliel's face and sees that he realizes what is happening. He says to Nicodemus in Latin, "The psalm says, 'When you send forth your spirit, they are created anew.'"

Mary Magdalene hears him from across the room and answers him in Latin, "God, Creator, Redeemer and Teacher." She shouts joyfully, "We have received a great gift—the gift of tongues." Saying this, she thinks, *And what will we do with this gift?* She remembers Jesus' words, *"Go forth and teach all nations, baptizing them in the name of the Father, the Son, and the Holy Spirit."* Immediately she realizes the value of this gift. *We'll be able to speak to all in their own language wherever we go.*

The crowd begins to murmur their wonder. Mary Magdalene sees the joy fill Miriam's face as she raises her hands to the heavens and shouts, "It's a miracle! Another miracle!"

The crowd picks it up as a chant. "A miracle. It's a miracle!"

Mary Magdalene watches Nicodemus and Gamaliel look at each other and smile.

The musicians begin to play their instruments and dance to a Jewish folk melody. There is radiating light around the faces of many of the believers as they interact joyfully with one another. Some groups hold hands and dance in circles as in a folk dance.

Mary Magdalene joins one of them. This prayer dance becomes a transcendent experience for her, filling her with an unaccustomed euphoria. She feels as if her very body is a prayer lifting her to the heavens and worshipping God as he was meant—fully with all her being.

The cantor begins to sing a hymn of praise and the people all join in.

He leads, "I love you, Lord, my strength."

The people repeat, "I love you, Lord, my strength."

The cantor adds, "O Lord, my rock, my fortress, my deliverer."

As the people are singing, Mary Magdalene notices that the nonbelievers who have not participated are simply standing by the walls and watching with awe. She sees an odd look on Uriah's face as though he is conflicted about what he is observing. Her thoughts are interrupted by the sound of Peter's voice.

Peter cries out, "The Holy Spirit is among us. Let's share our joy with others."

Mary Magdalene follows as he leads the congregation down the stairs.

Chapter Twelve

*A*FTER MOST OF the crowd has left, Mary Magdalene surveys the wreckage of the room, the physical testimony of the wondrous experience they have all shared. *Do I feel different?* she asks herself. *Only in the knowledge that life for me will never be the same.* Mary of Bethany and Esther grab her hand and pull her excitedly after them, down the outside stairs, and into the street, mixing with the pilgrims from other nations who have come for Pentecost. The followers speak joyfully to them of the wonders of God in their own languages.

Mary Magdalene speaks to a Roman woman in Latin, clasping the woman's hands in hers.

"Proclaim with me the greatness of the Mighty One!"

She turns and hears Mary of Bethany speak to a Syrian man. "I seek the Lord, and he answers me and frees me from my fears."

The women rush forward to catch up with Mary of Nazareth,

who is speaking to a young Egyptian woman.

"The Holy One is our help and shield; our hearts rejoice in him."

Mary Magdalene watches the Egyptian woman's shocked face as she says to her companion. "Aren't these all Galileans? Why are we hearing them talk in our own mother tongue?"

The other replies, "I heard them speak to a Roman woman in Latin."

Mary Magdalene looks around her at the faces of pilgrims showing much amazement but she also hears some jeering, including the loud voice of one man.

"They are full of new wine!"

A second man chimes in, "They're drunk!"

When they reach the temple, Peter ascends the first flight of stairs and turn to face the crowd below. Mary Magdalene marvels that he now speaks with eloquence and ease.

"Listen all of you. These people are not drunk. It's only nine o'clock in the morning."

The first man laughs and points to the disciples, saying, "They look drunk to me!"

"The prophet Joel predicted that God would send his Holy Spirit."

The second man jeers, "You expect us to believe that's happened!"

"Brothers and sisters, David predicted that a descendant of his would be the Messiah and that he would rise from the dead."

Mary Magdalene hears Mara, John Mark's mother, affirm, "He did."

"He was speaking of Jesus."

A third man cries out, "Jesus was crucified!"

"But he rose from the dead and now sits at the right hand of God."

The first man objects, "That's blasphemy!"

"The people you see here witnessed this."

John Mark begs the crowd, "Listen to him."

Stephen argues, "Is it not a miracle that each one of us hears this man in his own language?"

The third man relents, "Brother, what should we do?"

With power in his voice Peter exclaims, "Change your life. Turn to God. Be baptized. Receive the gifts of the Holy Spirit."

The first woman asks, "When can we be baptized?"

"Today!"

Now the first man who was so against these Jesus followers asks, "Where?"

"In the temple pool! Follow me."

Mary Magdalene moves closer to Peter as he heads for the temple pool, and the crowd follows. She watches Peter pass a beggar, who holds out his arms to him, "Master! Master!"

Peter stops and speaks to the man, "I haven't got any money, but I'll give you what I have. In the name of Jesus, walk!" Mary

Magdalene smiles as Peter takes the man by the hand and helps him to stand up. The beggar stands and then walks. Peter grins jubilantly.

"Thanks be to God!"

The crowd grows wild with excitement over witnessing yet another miracle. Mary Magdalene sees the beggar join them. As they pass the moneychangers and sellers of animals and birds for sacrifice, the followers crash against their booths sending money, goods, animals, and birds flying in all directions. She hears the vendors scream invectives at members of the crowd as they try to pick up their money and lost goods.

Mary Magdalene and the women stop and look at one another with alarm at the mayhem the crowd is causing. She sees a group of priests standing on the top of the highest flight of temple stairs and looking down on what is happening. *They will never stand for this,* she thinks.

The crowd surges forward. The pool attendant, seeing the masses moving toward him, flees. As Peter reaches the pool, Mary Magdalene watches him stand in the water and begin to baptize members of the crowd by pouring water over them.

"I baptize you in the name of the Father, the Son, and the Holy Spirit."

As each person gets baptized, he or she moves forward out of the pool, allowing another to take his or her place. Mary Magdalene watches this and then anxiously looks up at the temple guards as they walk along the periphery of the crowd. She sees Silas with them, which fills her with even greater anxiety. She thinks, *If he's here, Saul of Tarsus must be nearby.* She sees Silas lean close to one of the guards, and together they run toward the high priest's palace.

*T*HE NEXT DAY at dawn, Saul, looking disgusted, and Silas survey the debris from Pentecost. Saul feels that all his worst fears are confirmed. *There's no stopping them now; there are too many of them. Locking them up won't do much. There will have to be stoning and crucifixions.* He abhors bloodshed but hates even more these contaminated Jews.

They walk to one of the pools.

Peering into it, Saul says, "Filthy! Their practices are foul. Those foolish priests worried about civil unrest. What do they call this?" Silas nods in agreement. Looking up at the sky, Saul says, "Well, let's meet them."

*A*NNAS AND CAIAPHAS are seated around a table in a room in the temple. Saul is pacing as he stares at them. *Weak, incompetent fools. This is their fault. Well, I'm not putting up with their stupidity any longer.* Abruptly he turns and faces the high priests.

"They'll go home, will they?"

The two men are cowed. Caiaphas answers, "What would you have us do?"

"Round them up. Imprison them. Stop them."

Annas whines, "It would be unseemly to use temple guards for mass arrests. One or two people yes, but—"

Saul says evenly in a voice that brokers no disagreement, "Ask Herod for his soldiers."

"$\mathcal{P}$ETER TOLD ME three thousand people were baptized yesterday," Susanna says excitedly to Mary Magdalene as they sit in Susanna's office the next morning and talk over the events of Pentecost.

Absentmindedly with her head resting on her arms, Mary Magdalene muses, "Three thousand seems a lot. I couldn't tell." When she looks up, Susanna is taken aback to see that her face is a mask of anxiety. "As soon as we reached the temple grounds, I worried about the guards and the soldiers. They could have come into the crowd with their swords drawn."

"But they didn't," Susanna replied. "Mary, I think you worry too much."

There is noise from outside the office. They hear Uriah and others talking then there is a loud knocking at the door. When Susanna opens it, two temple guards seize her.

"You're under arrest by order of the Sanhedrin."

Mary Magdalene grabs one of the guard's arms, and he hits her hard with his forearm on the face. She loses her balance and falls. *And so is this how it's to end? Or is it the beginning?* They jostle Susanna out to the courtyard, where a number of other temple guards are waiting.

Susanna protests loudly, "You have no right!" The guard twists her arm hard behind her back. "Stop! You're hurting me!"

$\mathcal{T}$HE OCCUPANTS OF the house—Miriam with David and Cleopas; then Mary, Martha, and Lazarus of Bethany from the ground level rooms; and lastly Mary of Nazareth and Salome from a second floor room—stream out in alarm. The servants exit, too.

Mary of Bethany cries out, "What's going on?"

As baby David wails loudly and Miriam softly cries, Cleopas says, "They're arresting her for giving us a home."

Some of the men hurry down the steps from the upper room and watch as the soldiers quickly whisk Susanna out the courtyard's gates.

$\mathcal{M}$ARY MAGDALENE, DISORIENTED and with her face bruised and swollen, comes from Susanna's office. Mary and Martha of Bethany run to help her.

Mary of Bethany asks, "The temple guards?"

Mary nods as Peter joins them. He asks that they all follow him upstairs. They begin to go, and Uriah follows. Seeing this Mary Magdalene wonders if he had been close to Silas. Could there be a connection? *I remember him hanging around upstairs at Pentecost when he should have been working below.*

"We won't need your help, Uriah," she says. "Busy yourself in the kitchen."

She watches him wait in the courtyard as they head upstairs and wonders if he will be in the kitchen when she checks on him later.

$\mathcal{T}$HEY ARE ALL gathered, tense, and strangely quiet before Peter and Mary Magdalene in the upper room. Mary Magdalene prays silently, *Lord, help us to make good decisions now.*

She speaks first, "They'll come for us next."

Peter agrees, "We must get to the safe houses as quickly as possible."

Mary Magdalene pauses in thought and then asks, "But what about those who will come here for the meeting tonight?"

"Of course," Peter replies, "they must be told."

"I'll come back later and let them all know." Mary Magdalene then glances at Mary of Nazareth.

"I'll come with you."

Peter thanks the women and then tells the group, "The families will go to John Mark's; the unmarried women to Esther's. I'll give each man the location of his house."

Mary Magdalene can tell the men are excited to have a plan of action. She now addresses the women and families.

"You must leave Jerusalem as quickly as you're able. Intersperse with the Pentecost pilgrims."

Miriam cries out, "Please, Peter, we want to stay in Jerusalem."

Mary Magdalene goes to Miriam, kneeling beside her, "It's not possible, dear. You must go home."

The tears course down Miriam's cheeks as she wails loudly, "We don't have a home."

At this David begins to cry.

As Miriam packs up their meager belongings in their little room and sweeps it out, she remembers all of the times in her life when she has been homeless and dependent on the goodness of others: losing a mother at birth; dealing with a father who was sick as long as she knew him, coughing up copious amounts of blood with great force and frightening her with his suffering; then at six being taken to Cleopas' house as his betrothed—his mother had been cold and distant while she had waited with them until she was twelve and could be married; meeting his Aunt Ruth and being allowed to walk to her tiny house that she had shared with her son, Elijah. Aunt Ruth had been the closest she had to a mother.

She had really educated her in the arts of womanhood—how to sew, spin, bake, and cook—and instructed her in her faith, talking at length about the prophet Elijah, after whom she named her son, and his mercy to widows like she was. Cleopas just teased her at first and treated her as a little sister, but gradually as he had understood they were to be married, he had become kind to her so that by the time she was twelve, she truly loved him and had been delighted that they would make a home together. His father had given them a little house in the family compound and had generously used her marriage portion to furnish it. They had been considered well-off by neighbors.

She knows she will never be welcomed back there again after following Jesus. *Where then? Where will we go?*

Chapter Thirteen

*T*HE TEMPLE GUARDS march Susanna from the jail
through the Court of the Gentiles past curious spectators
as they leave the morning services. She, the widow of one
of the most successful, respected men in Jerusalem, feels totally
humiliated. Some people jeer as she passes; others snicker. Gratefully
she sees the compassionate eyes of a beloved friend, a woman whom
she hadn't seen for years, no doubt because of pressure from her
family. Their glances lock, and she draws strength from knowing
that this woman loves her and feels her pain.

Finally they reach the moment she has dreaded throughout
that long, miserable night when she must walk through the great
doors into the Hall of Polished Stones, named for its ancient stone
floor that has been polished through years of wear. This room—the
meeting place of the Sanhedrin—is the oldest part of the temple,
dating from the time of King Jannaeus. Two sides of the room are

curtained; the third contains a huge door through which members of the Sanhedrin pass from inside the temple.

Susanna feels ashamed of the wrinkled robe she is wearing and her disheveled hair. The guards had provided her with no means of grooming herself after throwing her roughly on a mat in the jail. Walking past the onlookers has been humiliating for her, but that has been nothing compared to the deep shame she feels now. She is facing some of the very members of the Sanhedrin with whom she—arrayed in all her finery and famous jewels—and her husband Solomon had dined.

She catches glimpses of men she knows well: priests, scribes, and doctors of the law, some of the most august men in Jerusalem. These men bow their heads before her. She sees that this is as embarrassing to them as it is to her. But there are others with crafty, cruel looks in their eyes that she knows are bent on her destruction. Seventy members of this tribunal sit on pillows arranged in a semicircle. The high priests Annas and Caiaphas are in the center. Their reputation is well known to her; they are seen as Roman appointees and are held in contempt by most of the men in this room because they are venal, grasping, and have grown rich beyond measure through their control of so many aspects of temple life. They are powerful, and few are willing to cross them. Solomon had talked often of the uneasy balance of power between the Sanhedrin and the Romans. Annas and Caiaphas rode the seesaw with assurance—Annas because of his many long years as a retired high priest and his son-in-law Caiaphas because of his consummate political skills. Solomon had guessed that Caiaphas and Pontius Pilate were close personal friends although neither man had done anything to display this. "Better to keep the façade as enemies, much better when you are playing both sides," he had said.

As she looks around the room, Susanna is counting on her personal ties to pull her through this. She catches the eye of her protector, who is careful to avert his glance once contact is made. She notices that among the spectators seated on either side of the room is a man matching the description of Saul of Tarsus, the one who manhandled Salome and Mary Magdalene. She suspects that he is her bitter enemy.

Caiaphas leads the tribunal in a prayer to start the proceedings and then calls witnesses who step out from behind the curtain on the left. Susanna gasps as she recognizes Silas and Uriah. Looking intently at them she becomes more afraid, worrying of what they might say. She thinks, *Mary Magdalene was right. How I wish that I had listened to her sooner.*

A scribe takes a seat at a table with papyrus and a writing instrument.

Silas testifies against her first, "Her house is filled with them: men and women who are followers of Jesus."

Caiaphas asks, "Will you swear to this?"

Silas says, "I do solemnly swear to God."

Caiaphas smiles broadly at the other members of the Sanhedrin and then looks to Silas for further confirmation. "So she houses them and feeds them, does she?"

"Every room is filled with them. They invite more people to meetings to hear their stories about Jesus. Three of them put up the money—the wife of Chuza, a Mary from Magdala, and this woman," pointing to Susanna.

"What say you, Uriah? Is it as he says?"

Uriah swears, "By the heavens, every word is true."

Susanna cries out disbelievingly, "Uriah, you too?" Uriah looks coldly at her, and she realizes that he has been her enemy from the beginning.

"Susanna," Caiaphas orders, "wife of Solomon, you are charged with aiding and abetting a seditious group, one that plans the subversion of our religion."

Susanna, with great dignity, replies, "We prayed and sang God's praises. How is that sedition?"

Caiaphas now turns his back to her and addresses the members of the Sanhedrin. "This movement was to end on the death of Jesus. Instead, his disciples preach in his name and foul the temple's pools with their practices." He looks from left to right at the members and then asks for their verdict. For many members her guilt is a forgone conclusion.

They call out, "Guilty!"

Annas stands and confirms, "She is guilty as charged." Turning to the scribe he says, "Do you have that?" The scribe nods.

"Then I ask that she be mercifully garroted until dead," Caiaphas intones.

Susanna shouts out angrily, "You have my Master, a humble and devout man, crucified, and now you look to the citizenry of Jerusalem to slay? You are the devil himself!"

Susanna's many friends among the Sanhedrin protest this harsh sentence by chanting, "No! No! No!"

Her priest protector speaks out now quietly but firmly. "The leader of this movement was crucified. It didn't stop these people, rather it has emboldened them, but they will have no place to meet now and many fewer resources. Her imprisonment will do more to stop them than her martyrdom, which may win her supporters and encourage them further."

Nicodemus now stands. "This woman is well known in Jerusalem. The wisdom of the Sanhedrin might be called into question if she were killed."

Susanna watches Annas rise. "I propose that her sentence be imprisonment for a year and then exile. Perhaps Damascus or Ephesus?"

The thought of exile is worse to her than the pain of death. She cries out, "Leave Jerusalem? Leave Israel? I was born here. I'll die here."

Caiaphas instructs the guards, "Take her away."

S AUL WATCHES ANNAS and Caiaphas exchange self-satisfied glances. They walk over to where Saul stands angrily. He can't believe the lenient sentence given to her.

"A year in prison!" he hisses at Annas, "You only gave her a year?"

Annas smiles cruelly. "She'll never last a year."

The rotund Caiaphas adds gleefully, "She likes her food!"

Saul looks from one to the other. "You're wasting my time! Tomorrow we round up the rest in that house or I leave!"

Saul notices the concerned look Annas and Caiaphas give one another as they remain silent. Finally, Annas speaks up, "Our appointment with Herod is in two days."

Saul says abruptly, "Move it up!"

"We can't do that," Caiaphas explains. "Just this once, we'll use the temple guards. Give them their instructions."

"I will and when I'm finished I want to see Herod. Understand?"

With this demand, Saul strides out of the room.

M ARY MAGDALENE AND Mary of Nazareth enter the courtyard of Susanna's house where a crowd is milling around. Some of the people, like Stephen, are familiar to the women, but many others are not. One young girl is being carried on a litter. Seeing her, Mary Magdalene's sorrow deepens and she thinks, *These people need us. Jesus' words sustain them, and Peter now has the power of healing.*

A woman spots them. "It's Mary Magdalene and Mary."

A person in the throng calls out a question, "Why isn't the upper room open?"

Another asks, "Isn't there a meeting here?"

Mary Magdalene breaks through the crowd, greets people as she passes, and stands above them on the stairs with Mary. The crowd surges excitedly after them.

A man in the crowd notices the battered face of Mary Magdalene and asks, "Who beat you?"

She answers, "One of the temple guards! For trying to protect Susanna. They've arrested her. Our enemies are moving against us. Go back to your villages." The crowd grumbles among themselves.

A woman speaks up, "We're not afraid. We want to stay here to pray together."

"You need to go home. Teach your friends and neighbors about Jesus."

Stephen, with great passion, answers, "Some of us are willing to die as Jesus did."

"If all of us are killed who will teach about the Way?" Several people agree that she is right. "Please spread the word that there will be no more meetings here. We're closing the house."

One asks, "Where will you go?"

"To safe houses. We'll mobilize."

There is great disappointment, especially among those who brought the sick to be healed.

A woman cries out, "We were hoping that Peter would be here and that he would heal our sick."

Mary Magdalene whispers to Mary, "What should I do?"

"Tell them you'll pray over them."

"But do I have the power to heal?"

"You have the power to pray."

Mary Magdalene closes her eyes and pictures Jesus with the sick and disabled. Strengthened, she tells them, "Bring your sick up. I will pray over them."

SAUL STANDS IN front of a group of temple guards in ragged formation and asks, "Who's in charge here?"

An older man answers, "I'm the captain of the guard."

"Did you arrest a woman named Susanna this morning?"

"I did."

"Go back to her house. Round up everyone you find and bring them back here."

A WOMAN LEADS her husband, one of the afflicted, through the crowd, "He's been deaf for many years."

Mary Magdalene places her hands on the man's ears and bows her head in prayer. "Father in Heaven, we beseech you, heal this man so he may listen to your Word and sing your praises." She looks up, continues to pray silently, and then removes her hands.

The deaf man looks around crying tears of joy. "I can hear! The Eternal be praised! I can hear." Mary Magdalene takes the hand of Jesus' mother and says, "He is with us!"

The crowd roars its approval, and another person takes his place.

$\mathcal{T}$EN TEMPLE GUARDS, now in rough formation, march through the Court of the Gentiles. The vendors and worshippers look with curiosity at this unfamiliar sight of guards marching like soldiers. They are used to seeing them at their posts.

$\mathcal{A}$ COUPLE PUT the litter carrying their daughter in front of Mary Magdalene. The girl is sixteen and paralyzed with palsy; her arms flail aimlessly, and her head moves from side to side.

Her mother tells the women, "She's like this all the time."

Kneeling at the head of the litter, Mary Magdalene looks deeply into the girl's eyes and lays her hands on her shoulders. While the girl looks up at her beseechingly, Mary Magdalene closes her eyes and prays silently. As she prays, the girl begins to cry—tears at first but then great racking sobs that shake her whole body. She rolls off the litter, writhing with the release of pain. First she covers her face with her hands and then moves them to her legs where she now feels life.

Mary Magdalene and Mary, on either side of her now, hold her. Mary Magdalene, her face translucent, looks down at the sobbing girl.

"She reminds me of myself when Jesus healed me," Mary Magdalene whispers to Mary.

Mary nods and returns her smile.

$\mathcal{T}$HE GUARDS ROUND the corner onto Susanna's street. One of them says, "There it is! It's that house!" They rush to the house.

One of them kicks open the gate and, spear at the ready, shouts, "Remain where you are!"

But then he frowns, and his spear dips. The courtyard is empty.

The commander of the guards shouts, "They could still be here. Search the rooms!"

The guards kick open the doors to each of the ground level rooms—empty. When they reach Cleopas's room, one of them spies a belt in a corner. Picking it up, he says, "Leather, I can use this!" Smiling at the other guard, he ties it around his waist.

One of them runs up the steps to the upper room and calls down, "None here." They try the front door, break in, go through the house, search Susanna's chambers, and grab what they can.

The captain stops them, "Careful, men, don't get caught with it. Saul's not going to like that we missed them."

One in Susanna's bedroom, with his back to the others, stuffs her remaining jewels into his pouch. The others try to fit larger items such as clothing and bed linens under their uniforms. Frustrated, they drop what they can't fit in their pouches.

SEATED AROUND A large table in a conference room in Herod's palace, Saul barely hears the chatter of Caiaphas and Annas; he's preoccupied with sizing up Herod, whom he's never met before. He recognizes that the big burly man at the head of the table is obviously annoyed at the intrusion and is trying hard to restrain himself. *He must be as wary of their power as everyone else is. Otherwise, why does he put up with this? Why would he have consented to move the meeting date?* He takes a hard look at Annas and Caiaphas. *I have underestimated them myself. They play on people like harpists, always striking the chord that will get them what they want.*

Despite his walking out on them earlier today, they were all smiles and charm as they rode here with him. They even offered him membership in the Sanhedrin and were pleased that he had all the requisite qualifications, including a wife and son. *Well, why not? I don't want to be in Jerusalem often, but it might serve my purposes to sit in that august body when I do come.*

Right now he is anxious to get to Damascus with the letters he requested from them tucked in his pouch—permission to round up the Jesus followers there and all the help he needs to do so. *My job should be done soon, and then I long to reunite with my wife and son in Tarsus. My family is taking good care of them, but I miss them. I miss working with my father and brother, using my hands to cut and sew. It will be a deserved break from all this.* He pictures himself handling the rough haircloth of goats and creating a tent. His father's greatest pride is that he is not simply a scholar but a man who can do many tasks. Then, with a stab of pain, he realizes that his father will plead with him once more to travel with him and sell the haircloth in distant cities, so that others can make tents of the same quality. He will have to refuse once more and explain that his brother Hiram is much better suited to trade than he is. His greatest happiness is studying the scriptures and the law.

His reverie is broken when he picks up that Annas is, at last, getting to the point of their visit and saying unctuously to Herod, "We're ready now to round up all of his followers."

Herod looks at the men quizzically. Caiaphas explains, "We need your soldiers."

Herod's eyes narrow, and he straightens his massive frame. "I return to Tiberius next week. My soldiers go with me."

Caiaphas pleads, "Just one company."

Herod maneuvers for advantage. "The Romans bear watching. I have friends who keep me informed but—"

Annas picks up on this. "We are your friends, Excellency, and we have sources within Pilate's palace."

Herod nods and asks warily, "If I were to agree, who would lead my troops?"

Saul says without hesitation, "I will."

Herod cocks his head at Saul, surprised that he would speak up. "Once you have them, then what?"

"Some will be imprisoned, some sent on their way to the provinces, and some inevitably killed."

Herod smiles. "Inevitably."

Chapter Fourteen

*T*HE SOUND OF rats scampering about the cell wakes Susanna. She bolts upright from the hard mat, fearing that they will run to her next. Seized without a cloak, she has nothing but a thin blanket to cover herself. The stench of the slop buckets fills her nostrils, and she longs for her own bed; the soft, fragrant linens; the embroidered coverlet.

Most of all she misses her husband's arms around her, the solidness of the man, and the way he filled her with peace and contentment. Perhaps if she just fills her thoughts and senses with the memory of him, this horror will be bearable. Her stomach gnaws at her, and she thinks of the gruel that will be her next meal. Self-pity floods her with the horrible realization that this will be her life for a year.

Now the noise is human: a guard unlocking her cell. Gruffly, he hands her a bowl, surprising her by saying not unkindly, "It ain't much."

She takes the opportunity to ask him, "Are people named Joanna and Chuza here?"

The guard looks outside to see if anyone is listening.

"They're dead," he says in a low voice.

Susanna, weak with shock, hands him back the gruel and puts her head in her hands. The guard relocks the door.

"No, Lord! No!" The dungeon is filled with her piercing shrieks.

*P*ETER WALKS TOWARD the temple with John and Stephen behind him. He knows how dangerous this is and that he's a wanted man, but there are no feelings of cowardice now because he also knows that the Holy Spirit is with him and that this is his mission.

Several people see them. One man cries out, "It's Peter!" Three of them fall behind John and Stephen.

They pass another group of worshippers. A woman among them recognizes him, "Peter. It's Peter." And she and others join the procession.

A voice in the crowd shouts out, "Perhaps there will be another miracle!"

As Peter moves forward, more people are swept up by the excitement and follow him. On his face is a look of exultant joy as he remembers his earlier cowardice and thinks, *Whatever happens, I will never hide in shame again!*

Ahead of him lies the Beautiful Gate, the most ornately decorated of the temple's seven gates. As they approach the gate, they are beseeched by vendors selling lambs that bleat loudly and doves in large cages that beat their wings helplessly.

The huge gates stand open, and Peter is surprised to see the lame man he cured at Pentecost at the entrance begging.

Peter grasps his shoulder asking, "Why are you begging? You can walk."

"I don't know anything else to do."

"You've been baptized! Come with me."

The beggar throws away his cup and eagerly walks with Peter. With the beggar clinging to him, Peter walks through the passage and out the inner gate to Solomon's Porch. As he always does, he stops to admire the magnificent view of the Mount of Olives and Kidron Valley. Striding down the portico, a pavement of colored stones and columns thirty-six feet high covered by a cedar roof, he sees crowds of men and women, pushing through vendors and moneychangers, come from all directions. They gather around him, stopping his progress.

A man, noticing the former beggar, asks, "Tell us how you cured him!"

Others in the crowd shout out, "Yes, tell us."

Peter turns to address them. "I didn't do it. The Holy Spirit did it in the name of Jesus," he proclaims loudly. "God raised him from the dead."

John adds, "Faith in his name restored this man to health."

As the crowd mutters among themselves in response, Peter sees three temple guards move forward. The lurch of fear in him surprises him, but he dismisses it. *If God be with me, who can harm me?*

One guard comes forward and seizes Peter. Another seizes John. As the guard ties Peter's hands, he tells him, "You're a public nuisance."

The crowd protests. One woman shouts out, "This man can heal. Don't take him from us."

Peter watches John struggle with the guard. John cries out so that all might hear, "You can't stop us from doing God's work!" A second guard is needed to tie John's hands. He cries out again loudly, "Jesus was a healer of many. He even raised men from the dead!"

Peter grimaces as a guard smashes his fist into John's stomach, knocking the wind out of him. He sees Stephen attempt to intervene.

"Take your hands off them!"

One of the guards slaps him saying, "You little maggot!" Stephen comes at the guard again. "Careful or we'll pull you in, too."

Peter looks up and sees two priests garbed in black walk up to watch the proceedings. *Vultures*, he thinks.

John regains his breath. "These people gathered here saw a man crippled from birth walk. They will testify to the truth of what I say."

"Stop this drivel!" one guard screams as the other guard kicks

John hard on the shins. "See, your shouting does you no good. Better come quietly."

Peter remains calm and addresses the priests directly, "Why are we being seized? Because a man who was lame from birth walks?"

The priests scowl. John answers Peter for them, "It's because the crowd listens to us and hears!"

One priest strides up to Peter, "You were warned not to teach or preach in the name of Jesus."

Peter answers, "I will never stop doing that!"

Two guards roughly move Peter forward.

IN A LARGE central room in Esther's house, the women—Esther, Mary, Mary of Bethany, and Salome prepare for a meal. Esther, dressed in a fine linen robe, directs the proceedings. She is very proud of her house, which is much better furnished than most others of its size. In addition to many chests for holding clothing, bed linens, blankets, and provisions, there is a large wooden dining table with six chairs made with wooden frames and woven straw seats. There is also a table for food preparation and, outside the house, a large freestanding oven. The women's mats are rolled neatly against the walls, and at night she provides them with blankets. Their cloaks hang on pegs in the wall. Two freestanding divans for lounging complete the furnishings.

Esther's bedroom off the main room is her greatest prize. The bed, mounted on feet and covered with an unusually thick, gloriously comfortable cushion, has blankets covered with silk from the Orient and an alabaster headrest. An ornate, carved chest holds her not inconsiderable wardrobe. Her parents left her all this plus a generous income so she can well afford to entertain her guests. She enjoys sharing her luxuries and is greatly gratified by the status her generosity affords her.

She admires her table setting with metal plates, knives, and ivory spoons. The other women, accustomed to eating on floor pillows and using their hands instead of utensils, took some time to get used to these luxuries. Tonight they will be dining on kid, vegetables, and cakes with the finest local wine to wash it all down. *I wish Mary Magdalene would arrive while the food is fresh.* Just then she walks in, but Esther sees her face is strained and full of fear.

Mary Magdalene blurts out, "Peter and John have been arrested for preaching!"

Esther feels her agitation growing because of this news. She goes to Mary Magdalene. "I thought they were supposed to go to a safe house!"

"Peter didn't want to stay under cover."

Esther runs into her bedroom and wishes Mary of Bethany and Mary Magdalene wouldn't follow her, but they do. Esther turns to them.

"I can't go with you to preach." She notices the look of shock on Mary of Bethany's face.

"Why?"

"Arrest, imprisonment! My neighbors don't even know I'm a follower. I want my quiet life back! I'm not going with you to Samaria."

Panic flashes across Mary of Bethany's face and Esther wishes she were braver.

"What about me?" Mary of Bethany pleads. "I can't go alone with two men."

Quietly Mary Magdalene says, "I'll go with you."

$\mathcal{P}$ETER AND JOHN pray, sitting on the floor of the jail cell, "Jesus, in your infinite mercy, deliver us." Silently, Peter wonders, *How will I fulfill my mission locked up here?*

Peter hears Susanna respond in an adjoining cell, "Deliver us, Lord, if it be your will."

Suddenly, the captives hear the sound of rushing wind followed by the sight of a dark, spiraling tunnel in the corridor. Peter hears the other prisoners scream out in fright as their cell bars shake. He knows only the three of them have seen this before and recognize it is the Holy Spirit come among them. Peter and John clasp each other in joy, and he hears Susanna shout out, "Alleluia." Their prayers have been answered.

Peter sees the guards, with their swords clattering at their side and helmets blown off, run for the heavy wooden door of the prison. Now the whole building seems to shake, and the dank, dark cells are illuminated with bright white light.

A tall angel, his face a flash of lightning and his voice as loud as a multitude of people, says to the three, "Go boldly and preach the word of Jesus." Motioning them to follow him, they are astonished to find that they have no problem moving through the bars of the dungeon and the heavy wooden doors of the prison. Peter sees the guards standing transfixed at the entrance, seemingly paralyzed and mute.

As they glide past them, the angel turns and again in a voice that seems to carry for miles says, "Tell the people about the Way."

He then disappears.

Peter looks around and discovers he and John are before the house of the men. He wonders if Susanna is in front of Esther's home, where the women are staying.

"Blessed be the ways of the Lord," he whispers in awe.

ANNAS AND CAIAPHAS are interrogating the chief temple guard in the Hall of Polished Stones. Other temple guards line the periphery of the room.

"Have you found out how they escaped?"

"We flogged the men. It appears they were all asleep!"

Caiaphas turns to Annas. "This young one preaching the resurrection of Jesus—we need to make an example of him!"

Annas nods.

"YOU STUDY THE scriptures, believing that in them you have eternal life. These same scriptures testified to Jesus and yet you refuse to believe!"

Saul hears Stephen's voice ring out in indignation as he harangues the crowd at Solomon's Porch, a very different group from the supportive one that Peter addressed just a few days ago. Saul sees among them are foreign Jews from Cyrene and Alexandria.

"Can you name a single prophet your ancestors didn't persecute? In the past, they killed those who foretold the coming of the Just One, and now in your ignorance and stubbornness you have become his betrayers, his murderers. Ask Jesus for his forgiveness!"

Saul turns to Silas with a smirk. "He'll be easily baited!

A man in the crowd calls out, "I believe in Jesus!"

Stephen tells him, "You do now because you've seen miracles!"

Saul calls out, "Tell us more!"

Stephen sees a group of temple guards pushing their way through the crowd. He speaks more rapidly now, and his voice rises. "Jesus died on the cross, ascended into heaven, and sits at the right hand of God."

"Blasphemy!" Saul calls out.

The guards have now reached Stephen and begin tying his hands behind his back with ropes. He writhes away from them, and says, "What you see before you is the persecution of hope and the good news of Jesus."

Saul says to Silas, "He's signed his death warrant."

Saul hears one of the guards tell Stephen to stop. A second guard hits Stephen on the chin with his fist.

"He needed that to quiet him."

As he is carried away, Saul sees Stephen look up at them and hears him say, "You can keep me from preaching, but you can't stop us all."

*M*ARY MAGDALENE, THRILLED by the miracle of Susanna's release, leans over and listens intently to her as she sits in a circle on the floor with the other women.

"I was freezing, and all they gave me was a thin blanket. And rats! I could hear their scratching all night long. It was terrible."

Esther shoots Mary of Bethany a look.

Mary of Nazareth asks, "But the angel! Tell us about him!"

"He was magnificent! His wings looked like white silk. I felt the power of the angel and the Holy Spirit helping and protecting us."

Mary, Mary Magdalene, and Salome all beam and nod.

Suddenly Susanna lowers her head, "I also have some terrible news." The women's moods instantly change. "Joanna and Chuza have been killed!"

Mary Magdalene remembers her elegant friend's arms around her that last day together and is sickened that the vibrant woman is gone. *How many more of us will die before the word of Jesus is spread throughout the world as he asked us?* she wonders. Then looking at her wounded sisters says, "We must say Kaddish for them."

Later that evening, black fabric is draped over the windows of Esther's house. Many candles burn throughout the room. The women, casting large shadows on the wall, sit barefoot on the floor in front of Mary Magdalene.

"May the Merciful One's great name grow exalted and sanctified in the world he created as he willed."

They reply in unison, "May his great name be blessed forever and ever."

$\mathcal{T}$HE SANHEDRIN SOLEMNLY files into the Hall of Polished Stones and takes their place in a semicircle around the two leaders. Saul, behind the curtain, feels a sense of self satisfaction. *At last we'll get somewhere,* he thinks.

Caiaphas instructs a guard to bring the prisoner in. Saul sees that Stephen's face appears radiant and serene even as he is led in roughly by two temple guards. Saul can tell that some members of the Sanhedrin are taken aback by his air of total calm.

Caiaphas begins the questioning, "What do you have to say for yourself?"

Stephen boldly replies, "You stubborn people are resisting the Holy Spirit."

Saul sees Caiaphas look back at Annas and smile maliciously. Saul thinks, *How predictable these fanatics are. They play right into our hands.* The members of the Sanhedrin look angrily at one another.

Unafraid, Stephen goes on. "You who had the law brought to you by angels are the very ones who have not kept it!"

Saul smiles as Annas steps forward and slaps Stephen on the face. "That's enough!"

Caiaphas calls Saul, the first witness. Saul steps out from behind a curtain. Addressing the entire Sanhedrin, Saul calls out, "He said Jesus was God!"

A number of the members of the Sanhedrin shout out, "Blasphemy!"

Annas declares, "We've heard enough!" Turning to the Sanhedrin, he asks, "What is your verdict?"

Saul hears one member without hesitation say, "Stone him!"

In a chorus of voices many of the priests repeat, "Stone him! Stone him!"

As the members of the Sanhedrin begin to file out, Saul walks to Silas, who is seated among the onlookers. "You said there were two. Point them out."

Silas points, "That one is Nicodemus. I've never seen the other one. Uriah said his name was Gamaliel."

Saul is stunned.

FILING OUT WITH the other members, Nicodemus and Gamaliel walk together. They turn a corner.

Gamaliel whispers, "Tonight I leave Jerusalem to visit my daughter in Tyre."

Nicodemus volunteers, "I have business in Ashkelon. My family will go with me."

They embrace and leave.

LIKE SUSANNA'S HOUSE, Mara's has a large upper room but that space, of course, can't be used to hide the followers. Unlike Susanna's house where the second floor is divided into numerous rooms, this house has a great room with much smaller rooms off of it, which makes it barely adequate for the families housed here. Despite Mara's best effort, her guests are not very comfortable.

After four days of confinement with so many people, chaos ensues. Children run amok, excited by having many new playmates. Their mothers try in vain to settle them down. Some children with sticks—among them is Joanna's boy—are laughing and running around people. Voices are raised as the adults' patience becomes frayed.

Two boys engage in sword play. One pins the other on the ground with his stick.

"Take that, you rotten soldier!"

The second boy lying flat on the ground begs, "Don't kill me!"

One of the mothers grasps the stick and breaks it in two. "Violence isn't what Jesus taught us."

In another part of the room, Philip and Bartholomew are trying to pray. Miriam is walking the crying David, cooing to calm him. Mara and Rhoda graciously circulate with a tray of jars filled with goat's milk. Mothers vainly try to hold children long enough to insure that they drink theirs.

A loud pounding on the outside door of the house causes everyone to freeze, and the room goes quiet. John Mark ducks out the back door and around the front where he sees Mary Magdalene and Mary. He immediately lets them in.

Mary Magdalene tells him hurriedly, "Stephen has been arrested and sentenced to death by stoning."

The news quickly speeds through the room, provoking general distress. Handing David to Cleopas, Miriam runs to Mary Magdalene. "Poor Stephen. He's just a boy. How can they do this to him?"

Nodding sympathetically, Mary Magdalene moves center and announces to all, "The women and children must leave Jerusalem at once. Go back to your homes. Teach your friends and neighbors about Jesus."

Miriam cries out, "No."

Cleopas, holding David, puts his other arm around her. "Don't worry. We'll go to my cousins in Cana. They have a big place."

Women cluster around Mary Magdalene. One of them asks, "Isn't there some way we can stay in Jerusalem?"

She shakes her head. "No, we don't want to take unnecessary risks. We have work to do outside of Jerusalem."

Philip takes Mary Magdalene aside. "Please tell Mary of Bethany and Esther that we'd like to leave tomorrow."

She replies, "Mary of Bethany and I will be back to go to Samaria with you. Esther has decided to stay."

Philip and Bartholomew look at each other in surprise.

$\mathcal{M}$ARY MAGDALENE THINKS how much Mary of Nazareth has aged these last few months. Her smooth face is now wrinkled, her shoulders stooped, yet she works as hard as ever. She watches as Mary takes two baked loaves out of the outside oven beside Esther's house and places them on a cooling shelf, replacing them with two unbaked loaves.

Mary catches sight of Mary Magdalene watching her. "I didn't see you there!"

Mary Magdalene embraces her and holds her for a bit. "Mother, I'm leaving."

"Where are you going?"

"To Samaria with Philip, Bartholomew, and Mary of Bethany.

Esther decided not to go."

Mary adjusts the loaves of bread in the oven. When she looks up, Mary Magdalene sees there are tears in her eyes. "Must everyone I love leave me?"

"I have to teach, Mother."

"So many losses."

They embrace again.

Chapter Fifteen

*S*AUL WATCHES THE guards march Stephen through the Sheep Gate to an open field worn to bare dirt and trampled by the many herds brought for sacrifice in the temple. As they bind him and force him to kneel, Saul looks at the thick walls that ring the city for almost three miles, walls meant for the protection of the populace. Now he, Saul, is like them, protecting the people from radicals like this man.

As the temple guards surround the young man and get ready to stone him, Saul of Tarsus, with the soldiers' cloaks at his feet, looks on approvingly. Another guard comes running on to the field. He tosses his cloak like a ball to Saul.

"Saul, catch this!" Saul catches it and looks over at Stephen thinking, *What has motivated him to throw his life away? What must have been the power of this Jesus? So powerful even Gamaliel, the great Gamaliel, is a follower.* This is one piece of information

Saul chooses not to share with the high priests. He loves his mentor too much to sacrifice him.

Saul listens as the leader of the guards instructs the others. "Pelt him hard! Let's get this over with quickly!"

Saul hears the crowd that has gathered to watch roar with approval.

One of the guards repeats, "Yes, pelt him hard."

Saul sees that Stephen kneels erect, his face serene and he is discomfited by such peace and certainty in the face of death. *These people have unnatural strength,* he thinks.

STEPHEN LOOKS UP to the sky. "I can see heaven thrown open." The rain of stones from the guards begins. "The Son of Man is standing at the right hand of God. Please forgive them, Lord!"

He hears the leader angrily shout, "Shut him up!"

A second guard says, "Aim for his head!"

Again the crowd roars approval.

As the stones hit Stephen's head, he says, "Lord Jesus, receive my spirit!"

PETER'S THOUGHTS ARE filled with images of Stephen: his inquisitiveness, his steadfastness and his foolhardiness, a fool for Jesus. He notices Andrew come in quietly and join the circle of

Peter, John, and six disciples who are sitting barefoot and silently praying. Among them is Manaen, Herod's foster brother, who has joined them undercover after the death of Joanna and Chuza.

The room in this men's safe house has been darkened, lit only by a single lamp.

After some time, Andrew tells them, "It is done. They went for the head."

Peter bows his head and pictures Stephen's beautiful face smashed by the heavy stones. Stephen was a son to him, to whom he gave a father's love.

"The Lord gave and the Lord has taken away," Peter replies. Looking around the room he thinks, *Stephen was the first, how many more of us must die before this movement fulfills its mission?*

The other men reply in unison, "Blessed be the will of the Lord."

*A*T DAWN THE next day, Silas leads Saul to one of the poorer streets in Jerusalem where the modest houses are huddled close together. The only signs of life are the street dogs foraging vainly for food and occasionally snarling at one another.

With a bucket of lamb's blood, Silas marks some of the doors with the sign of the cross. As blood drips down a door, Saul thinks, *We'll round them up, scourge them, force them to recant, and, if they won't, we'll kill them. Simple as that.* Deep down his stomach twists because he knows inwardly it won't be that simple. *Many of them, like Stephen, will choose to die rather than abjure their faith. I have dealt with dissidents before, but none as staunchly committed as these people.*

*M*ARY MAGDALENE TURNS her back to hide her tears after kissing Mary of Nazareth one last time. Mary of Bethany joins her and they force themselves not to look back at them, the women they are leaving.

With their arms around each other, Mary of Nazareth, Susanna, and Salome watch the two Marys recede into the distance.

Susanna pleads, "Let's leave, too. Please let's go to my farm."

Mary says wistfully, "Ein Kerem is where my cousin Elizabeth lived."

*A*T JOHN MARK'S house the visitors are hurriedly preparing to leave. Mothers are feeding babies and children. Fathers are gathering up the families' belongings. Martha, Lazarus, Philip, and Bartholomew move among the groups and pray over them.

Cleopas, Miriam, and David say their goodbyes and thanks to Mara, John Mark's mother. Miriam hugs the older woman tightly, and they leave. As a second family is taking its leave, Cleopas hurriedly returns.

"Your outside door is marked with a cross in blood!"

Mara and Cleopas examine the cross, which has bloody drips. Their faces are masks of shock and alarm.

Cleopas advises them, "You and your family better leave."

Mara replies, "When everyone else has left."

$\mathcal{A}$T DAYBREAK, A group of Herod's soldiers led by Saul kicks down the door of one of the marked houses. Saul feels a rush of excitement. *My task here will soon be over.*

They awaken the family from a peaceful sleep. The woman screams; the children cry. Saul oversees as the soldiers roughly pull the man from his mat and push him outside. The woman clutches at Saul's elbow.

"Why?"

He shrugs her off. He watches the soldier ties the man's hands and push him along the street to the next marked house. They kick that door in.

$\mathcal{M}$ARA AND JOHN Mark are at the door of their house hurriedly saying goodbye to another family.

Mara advises them, "Cleopas is headed for the Gate of the Gardens. Why don't you use the Sheep Gate?"

A FEW STREETS over, the soldiers kick down the door of another marked house.

PHILIP AND BARTHOLOMEW take their leave, murmuring thanks and warmly embracing John Mark and his mother.

IT IS NOW early morning. The soldiers have a large group of men, whom they are pushing forward around a corner to another street.

As Mary Magdalene and Mary of Bethany walk toward the soldiers and their prisoners, they realize that the arrests have begun and that they are in real danger. They see Philip and Bartholomew in the distance. Mary Magdalene nudges Mary of Bethany and whispers, "If only we can reach them before the soldiers see us."

Suddenly the captives and the soldiers turn the corner toward John Mark's house. Taking Mary of Bethany by the hand, Mary Magdalene slips into the alley between two houses.

PHILIP AND BARTHOLOMEW see the soldiers, Saul, and their captives. The two men stop by the side of the road, bow their heads, and don't look at the soldiers and captives as they pass.

They see the face of one of the captives light up in recognition of them, and then he lowers his head.

$\mathcal{M}$ARA EXITS HER house with two of her younger sons and Joanna's boy, who wonders where he will sleep tonight. Behind the house, John Mark leads a donkey laden with bundles. Rhoda is behind him carrying more.

$\mathcal{P}$HILIP AND BARTHOLOMEW are walking quickly. As they move past, Mary Magdalene and Mary of Bethany with their shawls pulled up over their faces come between the houses and join them. Philip doesn't acknowledge them.

Speaking in a low voice, he says, "We're headed for the Fish Gate."

$\mathcal{S}$AUL LOOKS UP to see John Mark's mother, her sons, and Joanna's boy exiting the house.

He lopes forward and yells, "Stop!"

Several soldiers follow. The family freezes in their tracks. Saul seizes Mara.

"You're under arrest."

"What have I done?"

"Supported a seditious movement!"

The soldiers tie Mara's hands behind her back.

Her fifteen-year-old protests, "Please don't! She's not well." He grasps Saul's cloak.

Saul picks the boy up by his robe and looking coldly into his eyes says, "Abjure this Jesus! Swear that you will not pray to him or speak his name again."

The boy answers, "I can't swear to this!"

Casting him aside, he orders the soldiers, "Arrest him as well and have him scourged when he reaches the prison. He'll change his mind."

John Mark now steps out between the houses and grapples with the soldiers who are tying his brother's hands.

"Take your hands off my family!"

Saul grabs the young man and punches him hard in the face. He falls.

Looking down at him Saul asks, "And you, will you testify that Jesus is a faker and a charlatan?"

John Mark answers, "Never."

"Seize him and have him scourged as well!"

The three of them are tied together.

The youngest son and Joanna's boy remain filled with terror and grief. Rhoda comes from behind the house, takes each of their hands in hers, and slips back into the shadows.

Saul turns to the officer with him, "Many of them will be running now. Send a man to each of the city gates. Have them tell the guards to close them."

Chapter Sixteen

*P*HILIP, BARTHOLOMEW, MARY of Bethany, and Mary Magdalene are walking toward Fish Gate. Mary Magdalene looks behind her, "What if we're followed?"

Philip answers, "I'll tell them we're heading for Damascus. We'll get off the road as soon as possible and walk through the brush."

"For Samaria?"

"For Samaria."

*M*IRIAM ADJUSTS HERSELF once more on the donkey that is carrying David and her up the steep hill of the road to Bethany. Even with the shawl holding David tied tightly around her neck, she feels uneasy on the incline. *Perhaps my nervousness is more than that,* she thinks. *Every step that brings us closer to our destination of Cana takes us further from Jerusalem and my friends. I've met*

*his cousins only once at my own wedding, but the family had
talked often about the miracle of the water being turned to wine
when his cousins were married. How I wish I could have been there,
but Simon, Cleopas's father, thought it would have been unseemly
for me, as Cleopas's future bride, to attend. Now I'm going to live
with these people. What kind of reception will I get? Cleopas says
they have a large place, and our extra hands will be needed. Will
I have my own little house again?* As her anxiety mounts, she has
a great longing to stop and look at the temple once more.

She begs Cleopas, "One last glimpse of the temple? Please."

Holding David, he helps her off the donkey, and they cross the
road to gaze. To her disappointment, the temple is covered by clouds.
Will we ever see it sparkling again like a jewel in the sun?

Suddenly, the sound of pounding hooves and blowing horns
startles them and fills Miriam with dread.

*C*LEOPAS QUICKLY HELPS her onto the donkey and hands David
to her. Looking down the incline on the temple side of the road,
he sees it is steep. The loud sounds come closer. He crosses to the
other side of the road; seeing that the incline on this side is equally
steep, he decides to stop and hold Miriam, David, and the donkey
steady until the Roman soldiers pass.

A troop of Roman soldiers bearing shields and horns round the
corner from the Bethany road and gallop into view raising dust as

they come. Cleopas's back is to them. He feels Miriam trembling with fright. One of the soldiers gallops toward the couple.

Cleopas is in his way, and he shouts out, "Move, you oaf!"

Cleopas has seen the edge of the precipice. If he moves, the donkey must move and Miriam and David will fall. He has no choice but to stay firm.

The soldier clubs him; the horses' hooves narrowly miss him as he falls.

Miriam looks up with horror and screams, "Cleopas!"

The Romans gallop around the bend of the road, leaving a cloud of dust behind. The sound of pounding hooves and blowing horns grows faint.

*M*IRIAM, HOLDING DAVID, gets off the donkey with great difficulty and goes to Cleopas who lies still. She feels his ashen face and neck and realizes there's no sign of life.

Covering his face with kisses, she begs, "Cleopas, darling Cleopas, wake up!"

The donkey tries hard to steady himself, wary of the steep incline. Frantically, Miriam places David belly down on Cleopas' stomach.

Sobbing now with grief and fear, she prays, "Dearest Jesus, bring my husband back!"

Cleopas doesn't move.

She cries out, looking up to heaven beseechingly. "You brought Elijah and Lazarus back! Please be merciful!"

With her arms outstretched she covers David's and her husband's bodies with her own. Her hand touches his. As she lies there silently praying, she feels Cleopas' fingers flex. Miriam thinks, *Can it be?* She raises her head and sees with amazement that his eyes are opening.

He asks her, "Miriam, what's happening?"

She gets up, laughing with joy; swoops David into her arms; and exclaims, "Thank you Lord. Thank you!"

$\mathcal{T}$HE CROWDS JOSTLE against Mary Magdalene as she and her companions get closer to the Fish Gate. There are farmers with empty baskets, merchants leaving with their wares, and several families. *The more people, the better,* she thinks, *they provide cover for us.* The people ahead of them stop to show the soldiers their documents as they pass. With a jolt, Mary Magdalene recognizes the large Roman soldier she met when going to anoint Jesus' body and quickly covers her face with her scarf.

It's their turn. As Philip and Bartholomew show theirs, the Roman guard asks, "Where are you headed?"

Philip replies, "To Damascus."

"Purpose?"

"I'm in the grain business."

He looks at the women's documents and then looks quizzically into the face of Mary Magdalene. "I know you."

Mary Magdalene's heart beats fast as she thinks, *Will it end here or will my bruised face save me?*

"She's my wife," says Bartholomew.

"She doesn't have your name," replies the soldier eyeing this man with arms that could lift a chariot.

"We just got married. I haven't had time to change the documents."

Groups of people are backing up behind them. The young guard reminds their inquisitor, "There are a lot of people waiting!"

Looking at the line, he says reluctantly, "Let them go."

$\mathcal{T}$HE FOUR HURRY through the gate, and the next group takes their place. Suddenly one of Herod's soldiers runs up to the gate and says to Titus, the brutish-looking guard, "Close the gates. Orders."

Titus balks, "Why?"

"Saul is looking for the Jesus followers."

Suddenly Titus remembers where he saw the woman. He recalls his hand gripping her hair as he pulled her head back and poured the oil she was carrying over her face. *How could I not have known her right away? The witch, always thinking she's so clever. Well, she won't get away this time!*

He turns to the soldier. "Four of them, two men and two women, just went through. They're heading for Damascus."

The soldier heads out after them, running at top speed. Titus turns to his young compatriot, Marcus. "Run and let Saul know. One of them is the woman he was interested in." Marcus reacts with dismay and does what he is told.

ON THE ROAD to Damascus, Saul's soldier runs past groups of travelers, examining each one for a group of two men and women. He spots two pairs and asks for their identification. They protest, and the women draw their shawls over their faces. As he examines their identification, three children run out of the brush at the side of the road.

"Momma, Papa, why is the soldier holding you?"

Shamefacedly the soldier realizes his error, and that he's lost precious time.

MARY MAGDALENE CAN still hear the noise from the road as the four of them run through a field off to the side, which is thick with brush. The bushes get in her hair and her eyes, but she welcomes the scratches as her fear of being caught gradually abates.

Finally Philip offers some respite. He spots some large rocks in the distance and points.

"We can rest behind them for a while."

SAUL, NOT SATISFIED with the hundreds of people he has rounded up, curses under his breath that he missed the leaders. *As long as they're loose, they'll attract more to them. And how many of them are still underground in Jerusalem? We must smoke them out! But first we get these four and make an example of them.* Suddenly he sees a Roman soldier running toward him, out of breath.

"The ones you're looking for just went through the gate, heading for Damascus."

Saul gives an order to four of his soldiers. "To the Fish Gate!" He sets off with them, riding as quickly possible through the crowded street. Saul is determined. *They eluded me once; it won't happen again!*

AT THE FISH Gate, Titus is attempting to hold people in both directions. Chaos ensues. In the distance, Titus hears Saul's loud cry to the crowd, "Make way!"

Titus calls out loudly, "You heard the man. Move!"

The crowd parts, and Titus watches Saul and the soldiers gallop by quickly, forcing travelers to hurriedly move to the side of the road or risk being trampled.

MARY MAGDALENE HOLDS Mary of Bethany up as they struggle on.

She whispers to her encouragingly, "It won't be long now. We'll be able to rest, perhaps even find a stream." The other woman is too exhausted and frightened to reply. She nods her head weakly.

Mary Magdalene is thankful that Philip and Bartholomew are ahead pushing their way through an area thick with brambles. They risk being cut by the sharp thorns to let the women through.

Mary Magdalene points to the large rocks that are much closer now with relief. "Look! Almost there."

SAUL'S PATH IS impeded by a large caravan of camels, carrying unwieldy bundles of goods. The camel drivers curse him as he forces them to drive their beasts off the side of the road. Pandemonium breaks out as one of the camels goes down, spilling and breaking apart the goods.

Saul doesn't even look back but gallops through the next herd, sending the drivers flying and barely escaping being trampled under the great hooves. Now the road stretches empty before him, and he realizes that he's lost them.

One of his men shouts, "They must have gotten off the road!"

Saul replies, "They can't have gone far!" The sweat is pouring off him as the hot midday sun beats down on him. The soldiers stop behind him.

"They were on foot. Look for a cutoff."

He turns back and rides more slowly now. The soldiers look

to the right and left as they ride. Saul spies a break in the brush. There! He rears his horse, turns in that direction, and dismounts to examine the cutoff. The soldiers follow. *The break hides a path.*

"Follow me," he orders.

The soldiers follow him reluctantly through the brush. The brambles scratch their bare legs, and they are sweating under their heavy breastplates and helmets.

Suddenly a great circular wall of light descends from the heavens and surrounds the men. Saul sees the terrified soldiers fall to the ground into bushes and brambles. They are stunned and confused, shielding their eyes from the brilliant light. Saul fights against the force, willing himself to stay erect and teetering to get his balance. He strains against the wall of light as he seeks an exit, but soon he, too, is thrown to the ground.

Saul looks up and sees a figure standing so close to him that he could touch the hem of the man's garment.

The figure speaks, "Saul, Saul why are you persecuting me?"

Saul answers in a trembling voice, "Who are you?"

"I am Jesus whom you persecute. What you do to mine, you do to me. Get up now, go to Damascus. You'll be told what you must do."

For the first time in his life Saul feels a deep humility. He understands that a new destiny lies before him, one that he will never shirk. The light now unravels, like a ribbon from a spool, and Saul attempts to get up from the ground. His head swivels from one side to the next, and he realizes, *I can't see!* He feels his eyes, shuts them, and opens them. He pulls himself up and then stumbles again to the ground, thinking to himself, *I'm blind! Oh, God, I'm blind!*

He hears Herod's soldiers run back down the path and cries out, "The light has blinded me." His terror filled voice rises, "Oh Holy One! What have I done?"

*M*ARY MAGDALENE IS relieved as they reach the protective rock, and she gratefully leans against it. She watches solicitously as Mary of Bethany sinks to the ground and, with tears of exhaustion, falls on the soft sand. Mary Magdalene strokes her hair to soothe her and notices that even Philip and Bartholomew have a look of great relief on their faces. She thinks, *How brave and willing they are to face every hardship.*

She smiles to herself as she pictures them in Samaria, walking into the town of Sychar and meeting the woman to whom Jesus spoke at Jacob's Well. She remembers how the woman had run from him into town and told the people about what Jesus had said to her. The people had flocked to him, had learned, and had been baptized. This will be fertile soil on which to begin their mission, spreading out from Sychar to the whole of Samaria.

Her thoughts drift then to the other Jesus followers leaving Jerusalem with the throngs of other families, merchants, and pilgrims:

Martha and Lazarus entering the small town of Bethany and Miriam, David, and Cleopas on their way to Cana. They and all the other disciples would preach and teach and spread the good news.

But to the ends of the earth? How will we fulfill Jesus' charge to us to travel all over the world? Even my imagination can't stretch that far. But I know if that is what he wants, he, the Man of Miracles, will have it done.

Her reverie is interrupted by Bartholomew, who says, "Someone is calling fairly close to us. We must be on the move." The three rise also listening intently. Bartholomew says, "It's a cry for help. Probably a ruse."

The women look at Philip, who apparently agrees with Bartholomew because he begins to gather their things hurriedly.

Mary Magdalene says, "Perhaps someone is in trouble. We can't ignore a plea for help."

$\mathcal{S}$AUL DOESN'T KNOW whether he is running toward the Jerusalem road or deeper into the brush. As he stumbles forward, he calls out.

"Help, help someone. I'm blind. I can't see."

He feels this is a punishment for his cruelties, one he knows he deserves. Yet his need for self-preservation is strong, and he makes his call for help at the top of his voice.

*M*ARY MAGDALENE HEARS it now.

"Philip, please, we must help this person. He's in some kind of trouble."

"The sound of the voice is coming closer, but the noise of movement is faint," Bartholomew guesses. "I think it's one man."

Mary Magdalene breaks away from the group and runs toward the voice.

"Help, I'm blind. Help me."

Mary Magdalene sees that the figure stumbling toward her is Saul and stops in her tracks afraid, thinking, *This is the man who would have us killed.*

Saul continues toward her, "Please help me. I've been blinded."

"How did this happen?"

"A brilliant light from heaven. I've seen Jesus. He wants me to go to Damascus."

Mary Magdalene closes her eyes and marvels, *Jesus is crafting his kingdom. I needn't have worried how it would be done.* She calls to him, "Come follow me. We'll take you to Damascus."

Epilogue

A S PREDICTED, THE baptized went back to their villages, where Jesus' teachings were met with joy by some and hostility by others. The first of many persecutions ended. John, Peter, and the other men stayed in Jerusalem for a time to preach. Then they, too, left on missions to spread the good news to all nations as Jesus had asked: some near and others as far away as Persia, Ethiopia, Armenia, and Arabia. On most of these trips, they were accompanied by women who taught and baptized women in these lands, just as Mary Magdalene and Mary of Bethany had accompanied Philip and Bartholomew to Samaria. Wherever these holy people went, they were blessed by signs, wonders, and great miracles.

Mary, Salome, and Susanna went to Ein Kerem. After some time, John went there to bring his mother and Mary to the Jesus community in Ephesus, but Salome had already died. Susanna finished out her long life in Ein Kerem.

And what happened to Saul of Tarsus? He became a follower of the Way. He went to Damascus, changed his name to Paul, and then traveled the world, preaching in Jesus' name. In his letters, he named many of the women, who were his coworkers and so important to his efforts, such as Prisca, Phoebe, and Lydia.

But would all this have been possible without the women who were there from the beginning of the Jesus Movement and who sheltered, nurtured, and led the followers in their own humble way?

These were the Women of the Passion.

Acknowledgements

I WOULD LIKE to thank those who provided me with advice and help on this novel, WOMEN OF THE PASSION: the Rev. Daniel Dymski who suggested that I write it; James Christian Peters, Vincent Robert, John Hushon, John O'Leary, Julie Lynch and Linda Reilly for their invaluable critiques; Ellie Richman and Maggie Fallon for their editorial advice; Landis MacIntosh who proposed the title and readers Peter Bukalski and Eleanor Erskine.

There were many others, friends and family, who encouraged me and read drafts of the work. Thank you all.

Through it all, from start to finish, my husband, Tom Lynch, was my constant support.

$\mathcal{J}$OAN D. LYNCH is a Professor Emeritus at Villanova University and the author of a non-fiction book and many articles. She lives with her husband Tom in Berwyn, Pennsylvania and Naples, Florida.